W9-CKM-130

AUGUSTA

*A Promised Land
Romance*

AUGUSTA

•

Carolyn Brown

Fic
Brown

AVALON BOOKS
NEW YORK

Published by Thomas Bouregy & Co., Inc.
160 Madison Avenue, New York, NY 10016

PRINTED IN THE UNITED STATES OF AMERICA
ON ACID-FREE PAPER
BY HADDON CRAFTSMEN, BLOOMSBURG, PENNSYLVANIA

To thebigsis, Doris Mead,
with much love.

Chapter One

Augusta Dulan literally gasped, grabbing her racing heart with her hands so it wouldn't jump right out the top of her red satin dancing dress. It couldn't be. Out of the hundred men standing on the other side of the road, hats in hands, eagerness in eyes, the first man to draw a mail order bride from the hat had chosen her name. She took a step forward from the middle of the crowd of women and the man who'd held her name on a small piece of paper looked like he could faint dead away. There Augusta stood in her red satin dress trimmed in black lace, the very one she'd worn when she danced at the saloons in Tennessee. She shook her head, the feathers of her headdress flying around her face in a flurry, but nothing changed. Surely she'd misunderstood. Heavy silence filled the town square as a hundred women and an equal number of men waited for the sky to fall in. Gideon Jefferson, the preacher, had just drawn the name of the former saloon girl from the hat, and he'd given his word that he wouldn't back down from the wedding.

"Well, it appears that fate has declared that the preacher will be wed to Augusta Dulan." Hank smiled and held his hand out to Gussie.

"I most certainly will not marry that woman," the

1

preacher declared, rage flowing from his eyes like hot lava from an erupting volcano.

Augusta abruptly turned her back, her face as scarlet as the dress she wore. She'd leave the rest of them to the ceremonies and she'd take refuge back in her wagon. What a horrid way to begin the whole day. They'd all been too excited to sleep the night before. Just plumb giddy with the preparations this morning, and almost shy when they'd taken their place in a line on the side of the road. It had been decided the preacher would draw first and then after he was married, he'd in turn do the ceremonies for the rest of the mail order brides.

Ninety-nine women turned around and commenced to follow Gussie back to the circled wagons. That preacher man had an egotistical, holier-than-thou attitude and if he wouldn't marry their Gussie, then none of them would marry that day. Gussie heard their soft whispers behind her and glanced over her shoulder. Their expressions said they were disappointed but determined. One more look at the preacher Hank had introduced as Gideon Jefferson left absolutely no doubt that he was mortified nigh unto death. His hands were knotted into fists of anger. His face, strangely handsome for a preacher, was taut with fury. She wondered briefly if he was looking at the same signs in her face and posture. Lord have mercy, she simply couldn't marry a preacher man. Gussie Dulan, a preacher's wife? That would bring down brimstone and fire from the heavens right there in the middle of the town square.

Gideon Jefferson's four young daughters sent up a howl when Augusta Dulan didn't step forward ready to be their new mother. Esther and Ruth, the six-year-old twins, sobbed into their hands. Four-year-old Abigail stomped her feet and glared at her father. But two-year-old Lucy put on the show. She threw herself down on the wooden platform decorated with an arch on the one end with fresh flowers cut just that morning entwined all over it. She screamed and kicked, tears flowing down her chubby little cheeks, and yelling the whole while that she wanted the pretty woman in red to be her new momma. Efforts from her father to quiet her were futile. Her sisters didn't help when they joined in the tirade, demanding that they have the pretty lady for their own. Ninety-nine men scowled at Gideon from the sidelines, and Hank chuckled. Who'd have ever thought things would start out on such a sour note as this, the culmination of all the past months of hard work?

They'd left St. Joseph, Missouri on the last day of April and traveled almost two thousand miles to Washington, California. A hundred men had paid to have Hank bring a hundred mail order brides to Washington. Decent women was all they'd asked for and Hank had screened his applicants well. He'd brought decent women. Even Gussie Dulan was a decent woman even if she was determined to wear her red dress for her wedding day. If Gideon would just listen to a bit of reason, but the look on his face said he wouldn't listen to angels if they appeared before him in all their radiant glory, complete with haloes and wings and a scroll with Gussie Dulan's name right on the top, sent straight from the courts of heaven.

"Get up and shut up or I'll take you home and put you straight to bed for the whole day," Gideon threatened Lucy.

She kicked him in the shins and screamed louder.

The mothering instinct in most of the women caused them to stop for a moment and turn around, to make sure no one had hurt that little spitfire girl. The men on the other side of the road looked absolutely miserable. Some of them kicked at the dirt; some slapped their thighs with their best Sunday hats; others shook their heads. Lucy kept up a steady howl; the other sisters sat on the side lines, making as much noise but at least they weren't flopping around on the platform like a fish out of water. Hank had a smile on his face that was more than a little strained.

"I can't do this. Not to that child," Gussie said. "All right, girls. Stop. We'll talk right here. I gave my word to marry whoever chose my name out of Hank's hat, and I'll do it."

"It's not you we're leaving for. It's that man up there who said he wouldn't," Berdie said.

"Let's go back," Gussie said. *Go back and face the music. I'll have to marry him or else all these past months will have been in vain. It's plain as the nose on a sow's snout that he don't want to marry me neither, but we'll get married. Later, after the rest of the girls are settled, I'll disappear. Maybe go back and live with Garnet or Gypsy. But now, I'll simply have to marry that preacher. Lord, please don't shoot a lightning bolt out of the sky and strike me dead when I promise to live with him until death parts us. Because I'm not going to, and that's a fact. Besides if I had to live with someone who hated me as much as his big old brown eyes say he detests me for very long, then death would part us. Right soon I'd be a widow.*

"Are you sure, Gussie?" Annie asked. "I feel so bad. If I hadn't asked to you to be the hundredth woman so me and Hank could marry, this wouldn't have happened. You'd be free to go your own way, wherever it might lead. I can still go and tell Hank we can't marry. Lord, girl, the way that man looked at you just plain made me sick to my stomach."

"I'm sure, Annie, and I wouldn't keep you and Hank apart for nothing. You were meant to be together and he'll be a fine father for Merry. Now let's go back and get this show on the road. Never was one to be late for a show." Gussie grinned, but deep down in her soul, her heart wept.

Relief washed over the faces of ninety-nine men when the knot of women returned to line up across the road from them once again. Augusta Dulan, in her fancy dress, stepped up on the platform, picked up the squalling little girl and held her close to her chest. All sobbing ceased immediately. The child nestled down into a bed of black lace that smelled like rose buds and sighed. She'd found her new momma.

"Okay preacher man, if you'll swallow your prideful nature and have me, I expect I can swallow mine and have you," Gussie said.

"Oh, all right," Gideon Jefferson threw up his hands in surrender. Those icy blue-green eyes on the woman gave him a case of the jitters. He'd marry the trollop. Not because he wanted to. God only knew how much he'd begun to look forward to a wife and someone to help with those four unruly girls his first wife had left behind when she died eighteen months ago. So why did God put that piece of paper in his hands with the name of the worst choice of the bunch on it?

"Well, now, I suppose we are ready to begin these ceremonies," Hank said. "Like I said before I will perform the ceremony to unite the preacher and the choice he makes from the hat. Then he will marry me and Annie. After that we'll go back to drawing names and the weddings will begin. I think we might need to do about ten at a time from there on out to get them all done by noon."

"I'm ready," Gussie said stoically. She'd walked the better part of two thousand miles only to find a surly preacher at the end of it. She tried to put the little girl down but Lucy clung all the harder to her, so she stepped right up to the arch with the child in her arms. "Let's get it over with. I reckon I can hold this baby girl and say my vows to this preacher at the same time."

Gideon joined her and the three other little girls on the sidelines, all wiping their eyes and noses with the sleeves of their rumpled dresses. "Hank, do the shortest ceremony you've got." His nose snarled back in disgust as he looked down at the woman he was about to marry. "Afterwards, you can go on home and I'll finish the others," he said to her.

"Afterwards, me and this child will sit on the sidelines and watch. I haven't walked for months not to see my friends get married. That's all they've talked about and dreamed about," Gussie said bluntly.

Gideon rolled his eyes toward the fluffy white clouds in the crystal blue skies. He'd have to train the woman to respect him as a man of God, a husband and just a man in general. The training could start tomorrow. Today, he had a full morning of weddings to perform. One thing was for absolute sure, even if God struck him dead, he wasn't going to stay married to that hussy. No sir. His first wife had been a saintly woman who knew her place well. That's what he'd hoped for this second time around and if he couldn't have it then he would have nothing. Augusta Dulan might be his wife on the paper, but she'd never be his wife in any other form. He shuddered as Hank began the ceremony.

"Are you sure?" Hank whispered to Gussie.

She bit her lip and nodded, never feeling more miserable in her whole life. The little girl sighed deeply, a quiver running through her tiny body. Gussie Dulan patted her on the back and wished she could cry and throw herself on the ground like the child had done. Pitch a fit like had never been seen before in the town of Washington, California. But she was a grown woman and she'd do her duty, even if it meant vowing to love, honor and cherish this man whom she'd rather be promising to shoot, bury, and forget.

"You?" He turned to Gideon.

The preacher nodded, using every bit of his willpower to control the frigid shiver making its way from the sole of his feet, all the way up his six-foot frame to the top of his head. "I'm sure," he finally said.

Hank cleared his throat and said the words that made them a married couple. "Now you may kiss the bride," Hank said.

"No, thank you," Gideon said. "Jack, will you sign these papers?" He asked the man standing next in line.

"You're supposed to kiss my new momma," Lucy complained, sending up another howl.

"Hush now, baby," Gussie patted her on the back. "It's

all right. We'll go right over there where I'll spread out a quilt so we can watch Annie and Hank say their vows."

"No, Daddy is supposed to kiss New Momma," Abigail stomped the wooden platform, the noise resounding like a gunshot.

Another one? Gussie looked at the other child. So the preacher had two children, did he? Could she claim fraud and get out of the marriage? Nobody mentioned that he had children. Or did they? Somewhere back in the attic of her memory it seemed that about the time Merry joined the wagon train, she'd overheard Hank say something about the preacher having children. She'd realized the tot belonged to him, but another one? Mercy, she'd just taken on a big job. Two children and a surly man. God might want to just give her a halo of solid gold encrusted with diamonds and other precious jewels for the couple of days she'll spend in that man's house.

"That's right," Esther and Ruth chimed in together. "It ain't real if he don't kiss the bride. Daddy, kiss her or we're going to start screaming."

"Oh, all right," he bent down and briefly kissed the woman's lips.

Gussie felt absolutely nothing. Just an overpowering numbness filling every fiber of her body. No heart throbs. No sparks or church bells. Not a thing. But her poor mind was reeling so fast and furious she felt a little faint. How many of these girls belonged to him, and what in the world had she just done?

Jack and Annie signed the marriage license as witnesses while Gussie took her brood of new daughters to the quilt she'd laid out before the fiasco began. In the distance she heard Gideon's deep, resonant voice begin another ceremony. This one for Hank and Annie. Merry, Annie's adopted eight-year-old daughter, reached across the quilt and squeezed Gussie's hand. A tremor shook Gussie's whole body but she squeezed back, her thoughts a rampage of disconnected ideas. Only one thing was real. Merry Wilson had her hand in Gussie's and that simple gesture was enough to give Gussie strength. Merry was the child that Willow, Gussie's youngest sister, had found abandoned on the trail. Annie had adopted her on the spot and now Annie and Hank, the wagon master, would be taking her back to Nebraska where Hank had a ranch. Through the months, Gussie had watched Annie fall deeper and deeper in love with Hank, who couldn't believe his luck at having someone like Annie love him.

In the beginning, when Gussie and her four sisters had joined the wagon train of brides it was with the understanding that if there were a hundred women when they reached their destination, then the Dulan girls would step aside and give the other hundred the husbands. When they circled up the wagons for the last time the previous evening, there was one hundred and one women. That's when Annie approached Gussie, telling her that she was in love with Hank and planned to go tell him, but only if Gussie would fulfill the bill for the mail order brides. It seemed like the thing to do then, but then she hadn't known the man who'd pull her name from the hat would be the preacher with eyes that flashed pure mad and who looked at her as if she was something he'd brought in the house on the sole of his boot after a visit to the hog lot.

"I'll miss you," Merry said softly.

"Me, too," Gussie said. "I'll miss you, but now you've got Hank to be your daddy and Annie is already your momma. You'll be in Nebraska on a ranch beside Willow and Rafe before long. Besides, it looks like I've just got four daughters so I bet I'm busy."

"What's your names?" Merry asked.

"I'm Esther and this is Ruth," one of the twins said. "We're twins and we're six. That's Abigail and she's four. The baby over there in New Momma's lap is Lucy. Her real name is Rahab Lucinda. But we just call her Lucy. Don't tell Daddy because it'll make him real mad, but we call her that because she acts like Lucifer."

"That's not very nice," Merry said, appalled at such a thing.

"Nope, it ain't, but it's the gospel truth," Ruth said. "She's got a temper like the devil himself. Maybe New Momma can do something with her. Daddy sure can't."

All the air went out of Gussie's lungs. Surely this was a nightmare. She'd awaken in a few minutes and the sun would be rising up in the east. She'd roll over and there would be Annie with Merry cuddled up beside her under the wagon. Just another normal day on their way to Bryte, California to find their husbands.

She should've known yesterday that nothing was going to be right. Last evening, when they'd finally reached their destination, they'd found out that things weren't what they were supposed to be. The hired hand stood up in the midst of the ladies and told them the story of why they were in Washington, California and not Bryte.

"You see," he'd scratched his head and tried to get the words just right, "the men folks had a mind to make their own town. A right nice town with new houses for all you women comin' so far and all. When Hank left they were working on a deal with a man who owns a chunk of land. His name is Bryte and they'd even told him if he'd sell off some of his land in lots so they could make a proper town with a church and all that they'd name it after him. Anyway, it was a pretty name and you all had already got used to thinking that you were going to Bryte so even though I knew when I joined up with the wagons that it wasn't going to be that way, well, I just waited to tell you. The plans didn't work out so most of the men decided to buy or build right here around Washington. So that's the reason you're not going to Bryte, but to Washington."

"Our mail? Oh my goodness, my sisters were told to send me mail to Bryte, California," Gussie had moaned.

"Not a problem. We done already told the mail business anything that comes to that address is to be sent down here to this post office," he said. "Towns folk's are right glad to have all the extra people in their town, I gotta tell you that. There's a big church with a preacher and all. He used to be a miner, too, but he's sold most of his claim and is now a full time preacher man. A school house with a teacher but you won't be needin' that for a while. Men folks, a few of them, have kids, so they go to the school in Washington. Got a general store, a bank and a lumber business. Most of you will be going home to new houses. All except the preacher's wife. She'll be joining him in the parsonage that the church people provided. It's right next door to the church house."

Gussie had thought at the time that it didn't matter where the parsonage was. She'd surely not be living in that house. Not even the Almighty would let that happen. After all, she'd been a saloon dancer, and God wouldn't want one of his own to be wed to a woman like her.

Evidently God had a sense of humor, she thought as she readjusted Lucy's head on her shoulder. Lucy had fallen asleep, her right thumb in her mouth. She certainly didn't look like the offspring of Lucifer, lying there like a wee sweet cherub with her chubby cheeks still tear-stained. However, her sisters had said she could be a handful and if that temper fit was any indication of what she was capable of, then Gussie had to believe it.

Names? Suddenly, she panicked. What were their names? Edith? No, Esther and Ruth were the twins, brown-haired girls with the biggest brown eyes she'd ever seen, sweet little bow-shaped mouths they'd apparently inherited from their mother because their father had a full, wide mouth that set in a firm line when he was upset. Abigail was the middle one, lighter hair, a mouth slightly larger, a combination perhaps of her mother and father. She had brown eyes, though, even if they weren't as ebony as the twins. And then there was little Lucy, with the lightest hair of all, and probably the palest brown eyes if the pattern ran true.

His name was Gideon Jefferson. That was branded on

her heart. Gideon Jefferson, the preacher man with the house right next to the church that she would never have to worry about. Gussie looked up at him doing his duty, talking in that deep voice. He was a handsome man all right, with dark brown hair with just a hint of wave in it and big brown eyes, more like Abigail's than the twins. Gussie's eyes fell on a good strong, firm chin, smooth, with no hint of a cleft to worry him when he shaved. A heavy beard was already showing a shadow even before noon.

The sun was straight up in the gorgeous blue sky when the final ten people stepped up on the platform to be wed. A slight nip in the air said it was fall, but it sure wasn't fall like she'd seen in Tennessee or even in the mountains during the journey to this place. Ice had crusted over the tops of the water barrel's attached to the sides of the wagons on more than one morning. Here in Washington, California, it was like a spring day, but it sure wasn't spring in her heart. It was dead cold winter, below freezing with a north wind cutting right down to the bone. Gussie Dulan's heart lay inside her chest, nothing more than a solid brick of pure ice. Gussie Dulan? She wasn't even that anymore. She was now Augusta Jefferson. She said it aloud in a faint whisper. It didn't even roll off the tongue right.

"New Momma, can we go home now?" Lucy blinked against the bright sun light and rubbed her fists in her eyes. "Lucy is hungry."

The crowd began to disperse, each woman being led to their new home by husbands either carrying their new bride's trunk or else hoisting it into a wagon or buggy. Whatever kind of home it was, it would surely beat the covered wagons they'd been living in for the past seven months. Everyone, including Gussie, had hugged Annie and Merry since they'd already packed their belongings and were staying in the town's only hotel that night. Tomorrow morning they'd board a stagecoach and get as far as they could before winter. Hopefully they wouldn't be stranded too long in any one place and would be back in Nebraska before spring.

Out of the corner of Gussie's eye, she caught Gideon walking toward the quilt. All four girls drew close enough to touch her, as if by drawing her near they could assure he wouldn't take their new momma from them. She slipped her arms around all four. If he thought for one minute he was going to make some kind of big male scene then he could think again. She'd had all the humiliation she could stand for one day.

A pang of jealousy zig-zagged through his heart when he saw her gather the children to her side as a hen would gather her chicks in the face of a storm. Well, they weren't her chicks, they belonged to him and him alone, and he could do whatever he wanted with them. He loved his daughters to distraction and he'd face hell's fires before he let a common trollop like that woman influence them in any way. Yes sir, he fully intended to keep a wary eye on her. Who knew what kind of folderol she'd be putting in his precious daughters' heads if he didn't.

"It's time to go home now," he said gruffly. "Come here Lucy. I'll carry you down the street to the parsonage."

"New Momma is going to carry me," she said. "She smells like roses. Did you smell her yet, Daddy?"

"No, I did not. And I'm going to carry you. Come here." He reached for her and she sent up a howl that would put a mountain lion caught in a steel trap to shame.

"Look what you've done," he hissed at Gussie.

"I didn't do anything. That child had a temper long before I came on the scene," she said, a sharp edge to her voice.

"You will respect me and never use that tone of voice again," he said in a hoarse, angry whisper.

"Respect is earned." She stood up without any help.

"I am a man of God," he declared.

"Honey, I believe you think you are a step up above that. But when you get through playing God you can fall off your pedestal and join us mere mortals." Gussie turned to the screaming child. "Lucy, your Daddy loves you so much and has missed you all morning. He would like to carry you, but I'll hold your hand the whole way."

"Don't you blaspheme like that," he whispered as he started off down the street. She was nothing more than what she looked: a loose woman with the morals of an alley cat.

"Blaspheming in your eyes, maybe," Gussie said, holding her head high. "Tellin' the truth in mine, honey. Don't grip so hard, Lucy, baby. You're leadin' me home."

"We'll lead you home New Momma." Abigail said as she grabbed her other hand.

"And us, too." Esther and Ruth filled their hands with red satin skirt tails.

Home, Gussie thought. She'd rather have been sleeping that night under the wagon in a raging thunderstorm out on the plains than in the house with this fool of a man.

"Your name is Augusta?" Gideon asked.

"You married me. You should know. My name is Augusta. People call me Gussie, though," she said.

"I'll call you Augusta," he said. "Gussie sounds like a barmaid."

"Imagine that," Gussie said, careful not to even touch his coat sleeve as she held on to Lucy's hand.

"Don't you get sassy with me, woman. I am your husband. You just married me," Gideon said.

"Yes, I did, but that don't mean I'll stay married to the likes of you. My name is Gussie and that's what I'll answer to," she said.

"New Momma is Gussie," Lucy said, nodding her head seriously. "I like Gussie, Daddy."

"Don't be calling her New Momma," Abigail said with a toss of her brown curls. "She's just our plain old Momma now."

"Not for long," Gideon murmured under his breath.

"Amen to that," Gussie said right back to him, loud enough that the girls heard it.

"See, I told you," Abigail said. "Just Momma. She just amened it. Like when Daddy amens after church. That means it's over. So now we can call her Momma and not New Momma."

"I guess that would be all right. What do you think, Ruth?" Esther asked.

"Momma sounds fine to me. New Momma sounds kind of funny, anyway," she said. "Here's our house, Momma. We got a surprise for you."

Gideon opened the door and marched in ahead of Augusta. He'd never call her Gussie. Not even if they hung him and dropped him naked into a six foot hole without benefit of a proper funeral. And he wouldn't treat her with the respect due the preacher's wife either. She was a common lady of the night and that's the consideration she'd get. He sat Lucy on the floor and the sight before him made him want to crawl in a hole.

Gussie took one look at the parlor and through the door into the kitchen and broke out in a giggle that rapidly turned into a full fledged roar. Gideon had never heard a woman laugh like that. It sounded like a man's guffaw rather than the laugh of a sweet southern lady. He whipped around, gave her a look that was supposed to dry up that foolishness, and was amazed when it just brought on more giggles.

"Drag my trunk in from the porch, Preacher. Connie and her new husband, Jack, brought it on their wagon," she said. "I think I'd better change out of my best dress and tuck my hair up before I tackle the cleaning of this."

Gideon did what he was told without saying another word. With strength born out of pure wrath, he hoisted her trunk onto his shoulder and carried it up the stairs to the spare bedroom at the end of the hall. She could stay in there until they determined just what they were going to do about this farce of a wedding.

"Love, honor, and cherish," he muttered as he set the heavy roll-top trunk beside the bed. "God, why?"

"Because that's what married people say," she smarted off right behind him. "A bunch of nonsense if you ask me. Now get on out of here, Preacher. I'm going to change from my fancy clothes, and don't worry, I won't wear my red dancin' dress to church."

"You surely will not," he exclaimed.

"Don't push me Preacher, or I will and if you don't quit treating me like I'm beneath you, I'll walk down to the saloon and offer to dance every Saturday night for free," she said.

"Don't threaten me, Augusta." He closed the distance between them until she was close enough he could smell the aroma of roses surrounding her. Wasn't that a joke—a barmaid who smelled like one of God's precious roses.

"Honey, I don't threaten. I state facts. Now get out of here, and don't ever think you can treat me like a child," she said.

He turned around so quickly that she wondered if she'd ever been looking deeply into those hauntingly handsome dark eyes. He slammed the door behind him and she plopped down on the bed, as she dropped her head into her hands and let the tears stream down her cheeks.

Chapter Two

"**E**nough wallowing around in a pity pool," Gussie told herself as she dug around in her trunk for a workday dress. She decided on the worst of the lot: a faded blue gingham check that the hot sun had bleached out to a near nothing color. It matched her mood and the numbness in her soul. She hung her fine dancing dress in the carved wood wardrobe in the corner and sighed. She pulled back the lace curtains covering a nasty window beside it only to find her view consisted of the cemetery behind the church. Fitting for the day she'd just lived through. All her hopes and dreams had died when Gideon handed Hank that piece of paper with her name on it. She even felt like she'd just attended a funeral rather than her own wedding. But Gussie Dulan, now Jefferson for a little while, was a survivor. Keeping that in mind, she pulled her hair up into a knot on top of her head, stuck a few pins in to secure it, and went down stairs to clean up the biggest mess she'd ever seen in her lifetime.

Gideon stood in the middle of the living room like a lost, bewildered boy. He didn't even know where to start. He'd banished all four girls to their rooms. The twins in one bedroom, Abigail and Lucy in another. Thank goodness the parsonage sported four bedrooms upstairs; at least Augusta could have her own room until this was sorted out. He and his first wife, Becky, had lived in a small cabin with a loft for the children up until she died. They'd had church services out in the middle of the yard for anyone who wanted to lay down their gold digging equipment for the Lord's Day. Then later they'd built a brush arbor. It was after she'd died and Gideon had brought her to Washington, where they had a church cemetery to lay her in, that the townspeople had offered him the parsonage and the church. Now he stood in the middle of his home wondering how one ten pound bag of flour could go so far.

"Where are the children?" she asked from half way down the stairs.

He looked up into the most unusual blue eyes he'd ever seen. With her hair up and wearing a decent dress, she looked down right presentable. A soft tingle brushed across the hard scars on his heart, but Gideon ignored them. He wouldn't let lust get in the way of good sense. Granted, it had been eighteen months since Becky died, twelve since he'd put his gold in with the other miners and sent away for a bride. But this woman was not acceptable to fill the role of a preacher's wife. Not even if she could put her hair up and wear a dress that covered her from neck to ankle. He'd already seen her true colors and first impressions were always the most accurate.

"The children," he said hoarsely, coughing to clear the indecent desire from his throat, "have been banished to their rooms."

"We just wanted to make a cake for the new momma," Abigail said from the top of the stairs. "And then Lucy got the bag of flour and started running with it."

"Go to your room." Gideon pointed toward the door, a hard, disgusted look on his face.

"Lucy said she's going to rip down the curtains and kick the window out. Then she's going to crawl out on the porch roof and jump off," Abigail said.

"Good Lord, she's only two," Gussie exclaimed.

"Yes, but she talks real plain. Me and Esther and Ruth, we taught her to talk like a big girl and not a baby," Abigail said. "I talk plain, too. We're not babies."

"Don't you use the Savior's name in vain," Gideon pointed his finger at Gussie.

She tried to focus her eyes on his extended finger, but it was so close to her nose that she saw two blurred visions. She slapped it away and took a step forward, putting her face right in his. Nose to nose, barely an inch separating the two of them, Gussie set her jaw and didn't blink. "Don't you ever treat me like a child. I'm a grown woman and you'll treat me as such or I'm out of here. I'm sure as big as this town is, one of those saloons would hire me in a minute. I'm so good at what I do, I can train a dozen other women to do a show in less than a week. So don't you tell me what to do or what to say. Understood?"

"As I said, don't you threaten me, woman," he said, his own dark brown eyes flashing a double dose of pure, passionate frenzy.

Too bad your passion falls in a bucket of mad instead of a pail of loving, she thought as the silence became a tension so thick she could scarcely breathe.

"Abigail, go get all three of your sisters," Gussie said without moving an inch. "You girls made this mess so you'll sure enough help clean it up. Besides we've got dinner to get ready and then supper to think about."

"Don't you usurp my authority. Those are my girls," Gideon said.

"And I'm their momma while I'm here," she said. "Just ask any one of them. Now, are you going to help with this or are you going to find something preacherish to do?"

"I'm going to my study," he nodded to a room off the side of the parlor. "When dinner is ready, send Lucy for me. Abigail, don't just stand there with your mouth hanging open. Go tell your sisters to come help Augusta clean this mess up. I should've known better than to leave you alone for half an hour."

Gussie set the twins to dusting flour from the furniture in the parlor and kitchen. She drug a cane bottom chair to the dry sink, slipped an apron around Abigail, and put her to washing dishes. She took Lucy with her to the smoke-house situated between the house and the outhouse at the very end of the lot. There she found a cured ham, two slabs of bacon, and the back haunch of a beef. Mercy, they'd have to eat a lot of meat in the next few days to use it all up and not let any go to spoil. She made plans to can the beef as she carried the ham to the house.

She figured they'd best have dinner before they attempted to finish the cleaning chores, so she set about peeling potatoes to fry, slicing the ham, and mixing up enough biscuit batter to feed six people. In between turning the ham, making sure the potatoes didn't stick, and checking the bread in an oven she wasn't acquainted with, Gussie managed to get the floors swept—if not mopped—and the rest of the dusting accomplished. A tintype on the mantle in the parlor left no doubt that *His Royal Highness's* first wife was a pretty woman and gave evidence of where the twins got their beauty.

She washed all four girls' faces and hands and then sent Lucy to ask her father to come to dinner. By the time Gideon arrived, she had the girls seated on the sides, herself at the far end, and had left a place for him at the head of the table. He sat down without so much as a single word for all Gussie's hard work. He solemnly bowed his head, shut his eyes, and gave a lengthy blessing over the food.

"We will have a late supper on this day only," she said, passing the platter of sliced ham to him first. "Since it is already two o'clock in the afternoon, I think perhaps a supper of pancakes and leftover ham would suffice."

"Pancakes with syrup?" Lucy asked as she bit into a biscuit filled with sweet cream butter Gussie had found in the pantry when she went looking for more flour.

"Yes, Lucy," Gussie said. "And after dinner, the girls

and I are going to clean their rooms and get a washing ready for tomorrow."

Gideon ate, appreciating each bite of the scrumptious meal. Slivers of onions flavored the potatoes, the ham was fried with a nice crisp shell of golden brown on the outside, and the biscuits were as light as yeast bread. Even if she was a harlot, she'd learned somewhere along the way to cook. Not even Becky could make biscuits like these, but then Becky had been perfect in ways this hoyden woman could never be. He didn't nod at her suggestions or make any of his own. He simply enjoyed his meal, wiped his mouth clean with the napkin she'd folded neatly and laid beside his plate, and went back to his study. He'd give her room and board; that was sufficient for her culinary skills. Praise produced pride and that was an evil sin.

"Daddy is still mad," Esther said bluntly.

"Mrs. Jackson should've come like she said," Ruth said. "Can I have another piece of that ham? I'm sure enough still hungry. Why do we have to clean our rooms?"

"Yes, you may have more ham." Gussie passed the platter to her, amazed at the way the six year old child could use a knife. Abigail had spoken like a prophet when she said none of them were babies. She'd only had to help with Abigail and Lucy's plates. "And when did you last clean your rooms?"

"Mrs. Jackson does it sometimes. When she has time Daddy pays her to clean the house, but it's been a long time since she had time. We usually clean up after supper. She was supposed to come by and keep us while Daddy went to the wedding thing. We was going to ask her to make you a wedding cake but she didn't come so we tried. But we didn't get it done, so we just washed our hands and faces and came to the wedding. Just when we got there Daddy pulled your name out of the hat," Esther said.

"I see." Gussie nodded. "Today is Monday. We'll be a day late with the laundry, but it will have to be done to-morrow. So we'll clean your rooms this afternoon, put fresh sheets on the beds, and get things ready for the washing. I'll probably iron tomorrow afternoon just to get it all on schedule. You two going to school yet?" She eyed Esther and Ruth.

"Yes, praise the Lord," Esther said. "We're already in second grade. We'll be seven on Christmas Eve."

"Why did you say 'praise the Lord'?" Gussie asked, a smile covering her face.

"Because if we weren't you'd probably make us help with the wash. I'd rather go to school than do that," Esther said.

After dinner, Gussie mopped the last remnants of the flour up off the wood floors which were in dire need of some rag rugs, which she'd hook if she stayed around that long, and in worse need of a real scrub brush and some wax. She sent the girls on upstairs to begin cleaning their rooms and was on her way up when the door to Gideon's study swung open with enough force that it would have knocked her down if she'd been a foot closer.

"I've something to say to you," he said, so close that the warmth of his breath kissed the soft skin on her neck. "There is a temperance meeting at the church on Wednesday night. You will be there. As the wife, albeit temporary, of the preacher, it is your duty, Augusta."

Her nostrils flared. Her face turned scarlet. Her temper took off like a team of wild horses—uncontrollably wild.

"I will not join a temperance group. I happened to have danced for many years in a saloon and I've seen what trouble those radical women can cause. If it were a women's rights group, I'd be there with bells on my toes and a song on my lips, but I'm not joining a temperance group to cause destruction of private property and attempt to force my views on drinking upon other people," she told him. "Now if I'm to catch up on everything you didn't do these past weeks, then I've got work to do. You go to the temperance meeting if you want this household to be represented. Or take Lucy. Most of those type of women would fit right in with a two-year-old with a healthy temper."

"You'll do as I say. I am your husband." Gideon glared at her.

"And for the time being I am your wife. That does not make me your slave, nor does it give you the right to tell me what I'll think or do," she said. *Lord, Almighty, who would have thought a wedding day would be filled with so much fighting and absolutely no show of any kind of love?*

"What's the difference in temperance and women's rights?" he asked.

"The difference is temperance is against the evils of liquor. They might as well stand out in the rain in their unmentionables and knock their silly heads against a brick wall. Men who are going to drink will drink. Those who aren't, won't. All the little pamphlets and fits those women throw won't change a thing. Women's rights are a different thing. We want the same rights men have. We want to vote, to own property. We want to be able to study for the law or to be doctors, and we want the same pay men get for those jobs," she told him.

"Well, dream on Augusta. That day will never come. Women aren't smart enough for those kind of privileges," he said.

"Don't kid yourself, Preacher." she laughed in his face. "Men wouldn't know the difference in an outhouse hole and a soup pot without women folks to take care of them. Women's rights are for educating men more than freeing women."

He grimaced, his fists balling up into tense knots at his sides. "You will be at that meeting if I have to hog tie you and drag you there by the hair on your head."

"Honey, you don't want me to go to that meeting. I'd have things in such an uproar you might not have a church to preach in come Sunday morning. And wouldn't that be a shame. Especially since it will be the first Sunday all the women on that wagon train will have an opportunity to sit in real church." She didn't back down one whit from his frozen scowl.

"And another thing, Preacher, I'd trade my front seat in heaven for a back seat on a barbed wire fence in hell just to see you try to hog tie me or drag me anywhere by my hair. If you ever lay a malicious hand on me, I will be a widow before daybreak, and you can drag out a stone and chisel and write that down for a pure fact. Now I've got cleaning to do. Have you got any other asinine remarks to make to me?"

"My sweet Becky knew her place," Gideon said in a deep growl.

"Your sweet Becky has gone on to her reward, and how great it must be for living with the likes of you." Gussie smarted off and stormed up the stairs, leaving him staring at her from the bottom.

What met her in the bedroom the twins shared made the flour-dusted parlor and kitchen look like a spick-and-span house on Sunday afternoon, all ready for callers. Dirty underthings had been kicked under the bed. The wardrobe had two store bought dresses hanging in it. For Sunday, they told her, and if they wore them any other day, Daddy got really upset. The rest of their clothing, other than what was on their back, was tossed all over the nasty floor. A fine sheen of grime covered the windows; the curtains, white at one time, were a dull shade of gray. Cobwebs as thick as her arm hung in all the corners, and the bed made her shudder. Sheets even more gray than the curtains and the quilt lay a tangled mess on the floor beside the bed.

"When did that lady you mentioned clean up here the last time?" Gussie she asked.

"I don't remember. In the summer time I think. She did go in Daddy's room last week and changed his sheets. Said he needed a nice clean room for the wedding time," Ruth said.

"Okay, girls, we've surely got our work cut out for us. What time do you get up in the morning to go to school?"

Gussie began piling the clothing, sheets, and curtains in a heap beside the door.

"Most times we just barely make it to school. Daddy hollers at us and gives us a cold biscuit to eat on the way," Esther said.

"Tomorrow morning you get up at six o'clock. We'll have breakfast, then I'll help you get dressed and fix your hair. Tonight you'll have a bath and I'll roll it up on rags," Gussie said.

Mercy heavens, last week she thought having Merry around was a handful. Now she had twins to get ready for school, a four-year-old and a toddler to watch while she did the washing and ironing, and an obstinate husband she didn't even want in her sights, much less one who did his work in the room right off the parlor. He didn't even go to work and stay gone all day.

"A bath on Monday?" Ruth was aghast.

"We only take baths on Saturday so we'll be clean for the Lord's Day," Abigail said.

"Well, you'll all have a bath tonight and clean rooms. Tomorrow these girls," she pointed at the twins, "will have their beds made and their rooms neat before they leave." Thank goodness for relatives in Tennessee who'd taught her the importance of cleanliness and routine. She shuddered when she thought of having to go into the preacher's room and remove his bed sheets, as well as wash his clothing. But that could wait until next week's washing, and who knew, by then she might well be on a stagecoach headed back to Frenchman's Ford, Nevada, where her sister, Garnet, had decided to leave the train.

"Okay," Ruth said. "We'll do it. You intend to iron our dresses for school too?"

"Yes, I do," Gussie said. "Now you two get this bed remade and I'm going on to the other room."

It was well past dark by the time Gussie finished her chores for the day. Supper was another scrumptious meal upon which Gideon made no comment. Even the hired help on the wagon train had the good grace to thank the cook for the meals. She'd had more compliments on soup and even pots of red beans than she'd had for two well-planned meals this day.

She'd cleaned, washed the girls' school clothes in a basin of water rather than dragging out the washing tubs in time to get them dry on the line before sunset, then ironed them by the light of an oil lamp. She'd started up a bowl of sourdough to make bread on Friday, which was baking day, and given all four girls a bath, then rolled their hair. She'd told them a bedtime story, tucked them in, and was quietly sneaking into her room when Gideon's heavy foot upon the third step from the top of the stairs caused it to squeak.

"I'll bid you a good night, Augusta," he said softly.

She'd thought his only tone was one of demanding gruffness. She nodded briefly and moved toward the door of the room he'd given her. At least the lady who came every sixth blue moon to clean had left her bed with clean sheets. Gussie would be doing laundry until well past noon on Tuesday if she planned to get caught up. It might take two bleachings just to get the children's sheets back to sparkling white. Even that would be asking a miracle of the bleach.

"You didn't expect me to sleep with you, did you?" He stopped at her door before she had time to open it. "I'd thought when I sent for a wife, I'd get a decent woman and I'd figured Becky wouldn't mind, if that was the case. But God would strike me dead if I ever . . ." He let his words dangle. Augusta was a lovely woman all right, but then most bar girls were. That's what brought the men folks into the saloons. Those men who were weak and didn't have enough faith to hold them in their day of temptation. Nobody had ever accused Gideon Jefferson of being a weak man, and he wouldn't be tonight.

"Honey," Gussie said in her purest southern voice, "God wouldn't have to strike you dead if you crossed that threshold. He might drop kick me into the next life for blowing the bottom out of that commandment that says, 'Thou shalt not kill', but He wouldn't have a thing to do with your demise. I'd take care of it with my bare hands. I don't want to be married to you one bit more than you want to be married to me. So you go on to your room and take the memories of your sweet Becky to bed with you. I'll just fall in a heap and go to sleep. Daylight comes early, and I've got two little girls to get ready for school."

"They don't need to be all dolled up, you know," he said hatefully, clenching his teeth. "Vanity produces pride and that makes a sinful heart."

"And filth produces something you don't even want to think about when they're teenagers. I'll bid you a good-night, Preacher," she said, opening then shutting the door so quickly in his face that he had to quickly step back to keep it from hitting him right in his aristocratic nose.

Gussie washed with cold water from the washbowl, then donned her worn cotton gown and snuggled down into the feather bed with clean sheets, even if they were musty smelling from having been in a closed room for months. The stars twinkled out the window and she remembered her sister, Gypsy Rose, always looking for secrets out there in the stars. And her other sister, Willow, who said there was something beyond the sunset.

She also remembered something the coach driver had said to Willow when she crawled out of the stage after months of riding from Mercersberg, Pennsylvania to St. Joseph, Missouri. She'd expected a small hotel at best out there on the edge of the frontier, but the first thing she saw was the Patee House, an elaborate hotel, right in front of her. The coach driver had told her that it was full up that time of year with people waiting to join wagon trains to go to California, to the promised land. He'd called them all fools because he said there was no promised land. Right now Gussie agreed with him. This place she'd traveled so many miles to reach wasn't the promised land at all. It was as far from paradise as hell itself.

Chapter Three

"**B**e careful Preacher," Gussie said, watching him gaze after his two daughters, strutting down the street in freshly ironed clean dresses, the curls in their thick brown hair bouncing down their backs below ribbons. They'd eaten a healthy breakfast and carried lunches of leftover biscuits stuffed with bacon in their lunch pails. That they felt pretty was evident in their giggles and step as they prissed down the street toward the schoolhouse.

"Why?" The smile faded when he looked back at his new wife. The night before had been a miserable one. He'd flipped and flopped all over the bed and had barely fallen asleep when Lucy came bounding in the door before sunrise, declaring that *Momma* had sent for him to come to breakfast. His girls calling her by that endearment came nigh onto gagging him, but what could he do. He'd been talking about their new momma for a whole year and it was too late at this point to insist they call her Augusta.

"Because I think I saw a bit of pride there in your face when you looked at Esther and Ruth. You know what you said about that," she told him.

"I'll be in my study working on a sermon if anyone needs me this morning, Augusta," he said abruptly and left her standing on the porch with Abigail and Lucy.

"Are we washing this morning, Momma? Can I help, Momma? I ain't big enough to put it on the line, but I can help, Momma," Abigail asked, loving the way the word Momma rolled out of her mouth.

Gussie remembered the rag dolls she'd found in their rooms when she cleaned the day before. If she could keep them busy and out of her way, she could get twice as much work done. Leave it to the good preacher to go hide away in his office. Well, it was probably where he needed to be— on his knees, getting some instructions from the Almighty about how to use his heart for love instead of bitterness.

"Me, too, Momma." Lucy slipped her small hand in Gussie's.

"I was thinking . . ." Gussie said seriously. Mercy, forty-eight hours ago she was just plain old Gussie Dulan. Now she had four little girls calling her Momma.

"I was thinking," she repeated, "that your doll's dresses probably haven't been washed in a long time. I bet they'd like some clean clothes, so why don't you two go on up-stairs and bring all of your babies down here. We'll take off their clothes and I'll make you a couple of washtubs in bowls and you can do your own laundry. We'll put an apron on you to keep your dresses clean and tie a clothes line between the back porch posts so you can hang your babies' dresses on it."

"Ohhhh." Lucy's eyes glittered.

"Can we really?" Abigail asked.

"Sure," Gussie said. "But first you make sure everything is picked up in your room. I'll come and make your bed later, after I get the lines full the first time, but I don't want to find a dirty pair of drawers thrown in the corner."

They both raced up the stairs and she went to the kitchen to carry another kettle of boiling water out to the backyard. She poured it in a tub and shaved a whole bar of lye soap into the warm water. She'd start with white things and work her way down to the darker items, finishing up with the few rugs she'd found beside the girls' beds. On Thursday, if she had time, she intended to wash all the curtains in the house and get them starched crisply. She wondered as she plunged the first dirty sheets into the hot, soapy water if all the other women were finding houses as messy as she had?

She ended up filling two crock bowls and two pans from the kitchen with warm water for Lucy and Abigail. Each of them had a corner of the porch to do their laundry, which they took very seriously. Gussie was amazed at the way they concentrated on the task and didn't lose interest. She wondered if she might begin to teach them their numbers and letters since their attention span was so amazing.

A warm November breeze stirred the sheets—which had miraculously become sparkling clean—and the girls' un-derthings, which desperately needed replacing. Gussie would have to start sewing things for them soon or they'd be totally without. She put her hands on her aching back and inhaled deeply. While the four lines of laundry dried, she praised Lucy and Abigail for their pretty washing hang-ing from the lines and told them it was time now to go in the house to start dinner.

"We'll help," Abigail announced, drying her wrinkled and pruney hands on the apron Gussie had stretched around her small frame.

"I thought maybe you could do something for me while I stir the beans and make a couple of cobblers for dinner and supper tonight," Gussie said.

"Pie?" Lucy's eyes twinkled. "Ohhh."

"I found a box of buttons in my bedroom. I have no idea how many are in that box and they're all loose. I thought maybe I could get some string and you could find the ones that are all alike and put them on strings for me. Then when I make new dresses for you girls I wouldn't have to dig in the button box. They'd all be right there, ready," Gussie said.

"New dresses, Momma? Does that mean I can go to school?" Lucy asked.

"Not yet, baby girl, but you think you could help Abigail work on the buttons?" Gussie hugged them both tightly, pushing back the curls from their foreheads.

"Yes, Momma," Lucy said seriously.

"Then set up to the table and I'll get you started on your job, then I'll do mine. When the washing is dry, we'll go back outside and bring in the dry things so we can put more on the lines. You can help me carry them," Gussie said.

Abigail announced that she'd found a bunch of buttons that all looked just alike about the same time that Gussie opened the potato bin and took out enough for their dinner. She'd have to go to the store before it closed tonight if they were going to have pot roast the next day. She grimaced. That meant asking the preacher if he had an account at the general store or if he bought from local farmers. That meant talking to him without fighting, and she didn't know if that was even possible.

"Count the buttons for me," Gussie said, checking the blackberry cobblers in the oven. She'd found a well-stocked pantry full of canned goods. Maybe they were left-overs from when "Saint Becky" was still alive, she thought, as she shut the stove door. Then a sharp prick straight into her heart stopped her in her tracks. That was no way to feel about these precious little girls' mother. Gussie remembered being an orphan herself, and how she used to find a secluded spot to hide away and just say the word *Momma* over and over again. Girls needed their mothers, and these four had been robbed of theirs at an early age.

"Momma, what comes after five?" Abigail asked.

"Six, seven, eight, nine, ten," Gussie said.

"Six, seven, eight, nine, ten," Abigail repeated, then started all over again from one, not missing a beat until she got to ten. Even if the buttons didn't match, she was counting them, making neat little piles of ten.

"One, two, free, four, five, six, 'even, eight, nine, ten," Lucy said, creating her own sections of ten buttons.

Gussie was amazed. The child had only heard Abigail a few times and already she'd picked up the sequence. "Smart girls," she said.

"Bragging on them makes them vain," Gideon said from the doorway. "And what are you two doing with your mother's button box? No one asked me if they could play with that box."

Abigail's lower lip quivered. Lucy sucked in a lung full of air to begin an ear splitting scream.

"It's all right girls," Gussie said sweetly. "I said you could count buttons for me while I cook dinner. Your father didn't know that, but he's not mad at either of you."

Abigail smiled and went back to counting. Lucy shot her father a mean look and picked up another button, ignoring him altogether.

"You are usurping my authority again," he said.

"I am doing what I can to make this place decent before I—" she stopped just short of saying the word *leave*, knowing that might set Lucy off in a tantrum. "And if it means two smart little girls counting buttons will help me get all the undone chores finished, then they can count buttons. Or if you don't like that idea, they can come into your hallowed sanctuary and you can preach to them," Gussie said.

"I'm accustomed to having a cup of coffee in the midmorning," he said, changing the subject. "I will forgive you for not bringing it this morning, but from now on you would do well to remember."

"You want a cup of coffee, then pour yourself a cup and get out of here," Gussie said. "We don't have time for you to be messing around in our kitchen."

Gideon would have liked nothing more than to slap the fire right out of her unholy cheeks. Standing there in her faded dress, her thick blonde-brown hair piled on top of her head, with her hands on her hips, telling him what to do and not to do, was almost more than his confused heart could handle.

"From now on you will bring me coffee at midmorning," he said, filling a cup halfway then adding boiling water from the kettle in the back. "I don't like strong coffee and I take two cubes of sugar."

"If I make coffee it's going to be strong enough to curl your toenails," she said. "If you want murdered water, then you get up in the morning before I do and make it the way you like it. I don't drink doctored up, weak coffee. And I've got enough to do around here without watching the clock to see if it's time for *King Preacher's* coffee. Surely you are capable of getting it yourself."

"Augusta, you are going to have to learn your place," he said.

"Preacher, I already know my place. You better work on knowing yours," she said.

The hot glares and stand-off was interrupted by a heavy knock on the front door. Gideon carried his coffee with him across the kitchen and the parlor. He opened the door to find Jack Haskell and his new bride. The woman, a pretty blonde with big round blue eyes swollen from crying, wrung her hands. Jack held his hat in his hands. The muscles of his jaws worked in tight little circles, and his green eyes were so bewildered that if Gideon hadn't known better, he would have sworn there had been a death in the boy's family.

"Gideon, could we talk to you a few minutes?" Jack asked.

"I want Gussie," the woman whimpered.

"Come right in," Gideon opened the door. "Step in here to my study and tell me what is happening."

"I won't without Gussie," the woman planted her feet on the porch and refused to move.

"What is going on out here?" Hearing her name twice, Gussie came from the kitchen, drying her hands on the apron tied securely around her slim waist.

"Not one thing you need to concern yourself with, Augusta," Gideon said.

Gussie could feel the heat and tension building like a

rumbling volcano at the front door. Connie, the youngest girl on the wagon train, and the one who'd instigated the most trouble, stood on the porch looking for all the world like she was about to explode.

"Connie, honey, whatever has happened?" Gussie held out her hand.

Connie rushed into her arms, lying her head on Gussie's shoulder and weeping uncontrollably. "I don't want to be married. I want to go home, Gussie. I shouldn't have come out here. I was wrong."

Gideon touched Connie on the shoulder, a fatherly touch, but she jumped as if she'd been struck by lightning. "Don't you ever lay a hand on me," she shouted at him. "You're all a bunch of animals."

"Okay, okay, Connie." Gussie soothed her by rubbing her back. "Let's talk about what is the matter. Okay?"

"He said the preacher could help," Connie glared at her new husband, who'd seemed fairly handsome the day before when he picked her name from the hat. She'd been nervous but everything hadn't been too bad until they went home.

"And I can, I assure you, Connie? Did I hear Augusta call you Connie?" He opened the door to his study and motioned for them to come inside.

"Augusta, you may go back to your chores," he said bluntly.

"I'm not going in there with the two of you without Gussie," Connie said, refusing to budge.

Gideon threw up his hands in disgust. "All right then, but Augusta is just sitting in on the discussion. She's not to say a word. Understood?"

Connie giggled. "Gussie, not say a word? I came here to get her words, Mr. Preacher Man. She's been the back bone of our whole wagon train for months and months. She and her four sisters have kept us sane and going when we would have laid down and died or lost our minds. So I'm not going in that room with you at all. If you want to take Jack

in there, that's fine. I'll go to the kitchen and help Gussie
with her chores and we'll talk while we do them."

Gussie could scarcely believe her ears. Surely Connie,
who'd caused Gussie and two of her sisters so much mis-
ery, didn't just say those words. Her wedding night must
have played havoc with her emotions and her mind.

Gideon rolled his dark eyes then drew his eyebrows
down in a scowl. "All right then, Augusta may participate
in the discussion, but what will we do with the girls?"

"They will be fine," Gussie said. "We can leave the study
door open and I can hear them."

The holy sanctuary wasn't anything like Gussie had pic-
tured. A big desk, covered in papers, was shoved in one
corner leaving barely enough room for Gideon to wiggle
behind it. Five mismatched chairs in bad need of paint and
new cushions were scattered around the room. The book-
cases lining the wall behind the desk were empty save for
a tin type much like the same as the one on the mantel.

"If you'll all sit down," Gideon said as he waved at the
chairs.

Connie carefully waited until Gussie was seated then
chose the chair right next to her. Jack fell into one as far
from his new wife as possible.

"Now what is the problem here?" Gideon asked.

"She won't be a wife," Jack blurted out.

"He's an animal," Connie said, wishing she could really
make him fall out of the chair dead as a Sunday dinner
chicken with her glare.

Gussie bit the inside of her lip and waited for Gideon to
stop blushing and attack this problem.

"The Good Book says a woman is to do her duties,"
Gideon said.

Connie turned her red hot frown on him. Too bad looks
couldn't kill. She'd take care of both of those men in one
fell swoop, and then she and Gussie could go back to Missouri. The preacher hadn't wanted to marry Gussie anyway,

so it wouldn't be any chore to talk her into leaving this godforsaken place if the preacher were graveyard dead.

"The Good Book says the husband should honor and revere his wife, treating her like a precious jewel," Gussie said.

Gideon's head jerked up so fast it made his head spin. "This is my job, Augusta."

"This isn't anyone's job," she said. "This is trying to help two people. Jack, where are you from?"

"Texas, ma'am," he said. "What's that got to do with it?"

"When you were in Texas, did you go to barn dances or social affairs?" Gussie asked.

"Of course," Jack said.

"And when you went to those affairs, how did you treat the women?" Gussie asked.

"With respect. My daddy would've taken me out behind the barn if I'd been disrespectful to a woman. Wouldn't matter if I was fifteen or twenty, he wouldn't abide disrespect to a woman," Jack said.

"And would you have danced with one of those pretty Texas girls and then expected her to fall into bed with you?" Gussie asked.

Gideon felt the heat rising on his neck. Surely his wife hadn't just mentioned two people going to bed together. "That will be enough of such coarse language, Augusta," he said after clearing his throat.

Jack grinned. The woman, Gussie, was a smart woman. He'd expected his wife to be as eager as he was since he'd been waiting a year for her to arrive. The idea that he needed to court her had never entered his mind.

"You should see that place, Gussie," Connie whined.

"Tell me about it. Is it too little? Too big?" Gussie asked. *Are the sheets clean? Is there a layer of flour everywhere?*

"It's a fine house but there's no curtains. Just the bare necessities. A stove but not enough cook vessels to cook a meal. And there's only one bed in the whole house."

"I see," Gussie said. "So Jack here left things up to you. He didn't want to put everything in there when he didn't know what you liked. What if he'd chosen purple curtains and you hate purple. He was just trying to make you happy, Connie."

Jack grinned wider.

"Jack, would you excuse me and Connie just for a minute. I want to introduce her to two of my new daughters," Gussie said. "But I'd sure like another word with you before you two go home."

"Yes, ma'am," Jack said.

"Now," Gussie said firmly when she had Connie in the kitchen with the door closed tightly. "That man is your husband, girl. And if you want to keep him out of the saloons hunting up another woman, you'd better learn a little about being a wife. Ask him if he's got an account down at the store and go there from here. Get the things you need. I've got a feeling none of these men we've married are paupers. While you're at it pick up a few balls of crochet thread and commence to making some doilies and such to give that fine house a woman's touch. Pick out material and make some curtains, buy ribbons to tie them back with. And get a couple of bolts to make yourself new dresses. You flirted like the very devil with Tavish O'Leary and Rafe Pierce. Remember when you dolled up that night and tried to seduce Tavish? You're not stupid when it comes to using the wiles of a woman. That man in there is plumb besotted with you, girl. It's that reason he couldn't wait to get you to bed. He thinks he's got the prettiest girl in the whole wagon train."

"I did not try to take Tavish and Rafe away from your sisters," Connie blushed.

"Oh, yes you did, girl. Well, have you thought about dressing up, putting a fine meal on the table, and seducing your own husband?" Gussie asked.

"What's 'duce?" Abigail asked from the table.

"It's something I'll tell you when you're old enough to know," Gussie said.

"I guess I never looked at it like that," Connie said softly.

"Sit down here while I check the beans," Gussie pointed at the table and Connie obeyed. "You've got all the right equipment, Connie. You are a lovely girl. Use it to keep your husband at home."

"I'd be mortified if he went to the saloon," Connie said.

"Yes, you would," Gussie agreed. "Now I'm going back in there and having a few words with Jack before you leave."

"What are you going to tell him?" Connie's big blue eyes widened in fear.

"To be nice," Gussie said, patting her on the back.

She marched into the study without even knocking in time to hear Gideon telling Jack that he was the man of the home and he should put his foot down with Connie. Show her who is boss and don't take any sass from her.

"I disagree," Gussie said, stopping right in front of Jack, her back to Gideon. "I think you should court Connie a little. Did you tell her she'd made a beautiful bride yesterday? Did you sit on the porch and hold her hand after supper? Did you kiss her softly on the neck and tell her pretty things in her ear like you did those lasses in Texas? Did you bring her a bouquet of wild flowers? What did you do to make your wife feel like a woman instead of a brood mare?"

Jack wasn't grinning anymore, but his mind was going full tilt. He'd been in demand in Texas with his charm and kindness. Where had they gone? Connie was more beautiful than any of the women back home, and he sure didn't mind the chase to get the game.

"She's his wife and a wife has duties," Gideon snarled from over her left shoulder. He'd left his desk and was close enough to her that she could feel the heat of his rage.

"She was a woman before she was a wife. Treat her as such. Do you want a wife who does her duty, Jack? Or do

you want a woman who loves you so much she can't wait
for you to come home in the evenings. Can't wait for you
to hold her or to tell you all about her day. You want a
wife to do her duty, or you want a companion for life? One
whose heart blends with yours to make one loving home?"

"Thank you, Gussie," Jack stood and extended his hand.
"I've got to collect my wife and take her to the store. Then
I think we'll have dinner at the hotel lobby so she don't
have to cook today. After that, I might need to pick some
flowers."

"You are welcome Jack. When you come in this evening
after chores, wash up at the kitchen sink instead of out in
the yard. And leave off your shirt while you sit at the table
watching her finish supper and let her talk about the curtains she's going to make for the kitchen or the parlor.
Show a sincere interest in what she's got to say, and she'll
return the favor," Gussie said.

"That's indecent!" Gideon all but shouted.

"A good strong muscular chest and arms might go a long
way," Gussie said, ignoring him.

"Thanks, again," Jack said.

They were getting in a snappy little carriage when Gussie
thought of something else. She hurried out the front door
and onto the porch. "Hey, Connie, would you put out the
word that the women from the wagon train will have a
meeting tonight at six. Right after supper, down at the place
where we circled up that last time. Women in town is invited if they'd like to come. But we sure want all the brides
there. Meeting will last only thirty minutes so they can tell
their husbands that. And we'll have one on Tuesday nights
as long as the weather is fit for the next few weeks. Girl
children can come with the ladies. Boy children will go
with their fathers who will wait for us right here in the
preacher's house and yard. We'll only be thirty minutes so
that shouldn't be a problem for anyone."

"I'll do it," Connie said. "Sounds like a wonderful idea

to me, and thanks, Gussie." She winked broadly. "Jack, darlin', would it be possible for me to buy one little bolt of material for a new dress. What I wore across country is all faded and ugly."

"Honey, you can buy six bolts if you want them," he said, looking back to slyly wink at Gussie.

"You are not going to any meeting tonight and you're not taking my children to a meeting where women don't know their place," Gideon said from the door.

"Who's going to stop me?" Gussie asked.

"I will," Gideon said.

"I don't think so, Preacher," she responded.

"Why are you having meetings with the women and you won't go to the temperance meetings?" he growled.

"Because those temperance women can take care of themselves. The brides are like sisters to me and I will meet with them." Gussie pushed her way past him back into the house. "Dinner is almost ready."

"They're my children, not yours," he said.

"Right." She smarted off and went back to the kitchen where Lucy and Abigail were carefully recounting all the buttons.

"Eleven, twelve, thirteen and fourteen come after ten," she had to work hard to make her voice pleasant.

"Whoopee," Abigail said. "Now we know more, Lucy."

"I forbid you," Gideon said from the doorway. " 'Wives, submit yourselves to your husbands', Ephesians 5:22," he quoted.

"Three verses down, Ephesians 5:25, 'Husbands love your wives as Christ loved the church and gave himself for it'. Being willing to love your wife and lay down your life for her—that's what makes a happy home, Preacher: Love, which begets respect, which begets harmony."

"Don't you quote scripture to me. You don't have the right," he said.

"Neither do you. Not until you do what it says." Gussie

took two steaming hot cobblers from the oven. She heard the door slam to Gideon's study and made herself a solemn vow that she'd be on the next stagecoach headed across the desert to Frenchman's Ford, Nevada.

Chapter Four

"We've only got thirty minutes so let's not waste any of it," Connie said as she stood up in the middle of the group of women in the grassy flat outside of the town beside the river. "Gussie thought it would be good for us to get together once a week so we could discuss things all together, kind of like we did on the train. She was a big help to me and Jack this morning. I think I can stay married to him now. Now that I've said that, I want you to listen to Gussie."

Gussie stepped out of the middle of a group of ladies and pulled her shawl tightly around her shoulders to keep out the night air. Back in Tennessee the idea of meeting even for thirty minutes out in the open air in the middle of November would have been lunatic. She could learn to love this part of the world with its temperate climate, even if she could never learn to love the man she'd vowed to love until death parted them.

"This can't be easy for any of us," she said raising her voice just slightly and keeping an eye on the four little girls she'd brought along. They played on a quilt with several other girls and seemed oblivious to what was going on in the meeting. "But things kind of came to me this morning when Connie and Jack came by to seek help from the

41

Preacher. We've all thought about the husband we'd get for all those miles and built him up to be some sort of prince or perfect man. Well girls, there ain't no such thing. They're just men folks, and like us women, there ain't a perfect one amongst them. But it does appear that they are sincere in wanting a wife even if they don't have the foggiest notion about how to treat one that just dropped out of the sky and into their laps. So I'm just going to tell you the same things I told Connie. I won't ask you how many of you are unhappy today because that's not the important thing here tonight. We all hope tomorrow will be better. The vital thing is that we adjust to our surroundings, and they're sure enough different, with husbands and children, than they were on the wagon train when we had neither, saving little Merry Wilson. I've been thinking that the wife sets the mood for the whole household." Gussie paused. Other than her own, that was. The preacher set the mood in their house and it was surly at best.

"If you're happy, then everyone will be happy. If you aren't, then it's Katy-Bar-The-Door and get the gun. What I told these two this morning is to be nice to each other. I think that's the answer to making a marriage work: Kindness. Say thank you when he does something for you. Tell him he's handsome when he's cleaned up for church on Sunday morning. Tell him he's got big muscles if he has them or pretty eyes if they are. Tell him you love the house he's built or bought for you. Ask him if you have an account at the general store so you can put feminine touches to it. Curtains, doilies. Women's things that men love," she continued.

"You think that will work?" Berdie asked.

"Yes, it does," Connie giggled off to Gussie's right. "Jack took me to the store himself this morning. He let me buy anything I wanted. Even the material for three new dresses, and then he turned around and bought me one of the two sewing machines Cecil had in the window of the store. When we got home, he helped me out of the buggy and after supper he rubbed my neck, saying that it wasn't any wonder I was tired since I'd worked so hard all afternoon putting away the new things he'd bought for me. He held my hand all the way to the preacher's house and even kissed me on the lips softly just before we got out. I think I might be falling in love with my husband after only one day."

"Kindness, huh?" Jenny asked. "But what if I'm kind and he's still standoffish and cold?"

"You can catch more flies with honey than vinegar," Connie said.

"Any more questions or comments?" Gussie asked.

"I want to go home and I don't mean home with my new husband. I want to go home to Missouri. This was a mistake," Viola said from the back of the group.

"I thought the same thing until I tried Gussie's plan," Connie said. "But you know flirting don't have to end with 'I do'. I think I'm going to like being married after all. And let me tell you, there's two saloons in town that have women in them who'll flirt if we don't want to."

"How many of you need a lesson in how to flirt?" Gussie grinned, noticing a flash of white in the brush behind them.

Half a dozen hands raised, unashamed, Viola's amongst them.

"Then I want you to make a little time tomorrow afternoon to visit with Connie. Take your crochet or mending along with you for a half an hour. Tomorrow, she will be home and most likely sewing on that machine. She can visit while she works. She's the new resident advisor in that area," Gussie said.

"Now how many of you cannot sew a stitch, even on your fingers? Or who's never used a sewing machine?" Gussie asked.

At least six other hands raised up in the air.

"Then you will visit Berdie sometime this week. She can show you how to cut the material or feed sacks into lengths for curtains and how to make them. I've seen her stitching while we were on the wagon train. She did some fine work on little Merry's dresses so I know she'll be glad to give you all some lessons," Gussie said.

Berdie nodded. "I'll be sewing my own curtains on Thursday. Please drop by any time in the afternoon. Bring your measurements and enough fabric to make at least one pair of curtains. I'll show you how to make them and then you can work on the rest at your own pace. I'm asking my husband, Will, for a sewing machine soon as I get home tonight. Guess that store owner better get ready to send in an order for a bunch of them, huh girls?"

"That's right," a chorus sounded amongst the women.

"Now how many of you got a ready-made family and aren't quite sure what to do with children?" Gussie asked.

Several hands went up in the air.

"I did too. Four little girls. I'm not so sure—since the preacher really doesn't want to me married to me—just how long I'm going to be in Washington. But I will be home any afternoon this week. Bring your children and we'll discuss how to take care of them, since this is new ground for us to be covering," Gussie said.

"Any more questions?" Connie asked.

"What do you mean, you might be leaving?" Viola asked.

"She's not thinking straight or flirting with her preacher man," Connie giggled. "We can't do without Gussie."

"I think that's enough for us to work on this week," Viola said. "Can we meet again next week? I felt like I was on an island with a storm rolling in off the ocean all by myself today. After having the girls on the wagons around me so much, the loneliness was more than I could bear. I didn't get a man with a child so I didn't even have that to keep me company today. He's stopped mining and is farming. There's cattle, and I'm used to the farming way of life, but living with a stranger for a husband ain't so easy. I like what you said, and I know how to sew, too. So if any of you want to bring your curtains to me, I'd be glad to help you."

"Good, anyone else?" Gussie asked.

"Well, this is embarrassing," Berdie piped up. "But I think the man I got is the prettiest thing I've ever seen. And he's sleeping in the loft he says, until I get used to being a wife. Connie, you really think that flirting will help? 'Cause I think I'm used to being a wife already."

What erupted from Connie was more than a giggle, more than a laugh. It bordered on a pure guffaw. She wiped her eyes, and threw her arm around Berdie's shoulders. "By Sunday, he won't be in that loft," Connie said. "And if he is, then I've done lost my touch. Now I think our time is up, girls. Let's go work on making happy homes."

"Remember it ain't perfect," Gussie said. "They're just men folks so don't expect too much too fast."

"Ain't it the truth," Connie said, leading the way back to the parsonage.

The meeting of men in the preacher's backyard had started out disastrous. Gideon took a stand on the back porch and told them all that they were the head of the household and to insist that their women be submissive. Before he could get wound up in a sermon, Jack spoke up from out in the yard and commenced to telling them what Gussie had told him that morning.

In a quiet, yet deep, Texas drawl he told them to be kind to their wives. The women had traveled a long time with few men in their presence and they were a bit skittish. You didn't break a colt by rushing it, but by tender loving care. He repeated what Gussie had said about a companion or a brood mare and several of the men laughed. Then he told them a couple of weeks of patience was nothing compared to the months they'd waited for the brides.

Gideon had heard all the nonsense he wanted to hear and eased out into the darkness when they started telling about their own personal experiences of the night before and their first day. He slipped through the trees to the brush behind where the women were meeting. Gussie probably had them all stirred up and ready to leave on the next conveyance out of Washington. He squatted on his heels and listened.

Had anyone been looking in his direction, they could have seen a red glow when the women started discussing flirting with their husbands, seducing them if you please. Wives didn't do that! They were grateful to have a home and children, both given to them by their husbands who remained faithful no matter what. His sweet Becky stayed in the background, doing his bidding, making his life run smooth. The day he came home and told her they would be taking their twins and moving to California, that he'd sold their farm and told the deacons at the church he'd felt God's call for him to carry the gospel to the miners, she had just nodded and began to pack. Gideon couldn't imagine Augusta doing anything like that. She would have argued for a month, then most likely set her heels and refused to budge. That's why he couldn't wait to be rid of the woman. Celibacy, with all it's loneliness, was a better alternative than living with a shrew.

He barely beat the women back to the house and had just slipped back into a group of men who were discussing an item in the *Sonoma County Journal* printed in Petaluma, California concerning the fact that the mail order brides had arrived in Washington and the weddings had taken place. The editor of the newspaper wished them all happiness and long and joyful marriages. That might work for some of these poor, helpless men, willing to set aside God's order of things, but it sure wouldn't work for Gideon Jefferson.

"Daddy, Daddy! We got to play with Winnie and Bonnie," the twins cried as they came running to his side. "And we're going to have another meeting next week, too. And Momma says we can go."

"We'll see." He patted the girls on their heads. By next week, with any luck, that meddlesome woman would be gone and there would be no more meetings. He'd just count the money he spent bringing her to California a lesson in taking matters in his own hands and not waiting on God to answer his prayers. Surely there was a good god-fearing woman out there who would make a fine preacher's wife.

Later that night, after Gussie had ironed dresses for all four girls for the next day, washed them up, dampened their hair and re-rolled it, and tucked them all into bed, she made one more trip down the stairs to check her sourdough starter. It would be a week before she could actually make bread from it. But until then they weren't having too big a problem eating biscuits for breakfast and cornbread for dinner and supper.

"Augusta, a word with you," Gideon said, hanging his coat on the rack inside the front door. "I will keep the children tomorrow night for you to attend the temperance meeting. You will, of course, have their nightly washing done and whatever it is you do to their hair before you leave. I will read them a story from the Bible while you are gone."

Kindness, her heart reminded her. She smiled sweetly. "Tell you what. I'll do all those things and tell them a story while the meeting is going on. I told you before, I'm not going. Not this time. Not any time." There, she'd listened carefully to her voice and it hadn't had a cutting edge to it. She'd simply stated facts and let it go at that.

"No man is ever going to marry a mule-headed, irritable woman like you," he snapped.

"You did," she said.

"I had no choice," he smarted off and wanted to bite his tongue immediately. Jack had said that he and Connie were getting on so much better when he flirted and courted her. But Gideon didn't want to flirt or court. He just wanted his life back the way it used to be. Nice and calm. Even if his daughters did leave for school looking like poor orphans, at least his heart wasn't in a turmoil of conflicting emotions all the time. He couldn't bear a year of what he'd just endured the past twenty-four hours.

"That's right, but I'll make it easy on you, Preacher," Gussie said. "The next time a stagecoach leaves this place, I'll be on it. You can divorce me immediately."

"Divorce is wrong," he said.

"So is marriage with no love," she told him as she made her way up the stairs to bed.

"Amen to that," he replied, blowing out the last lamp before he went up to his own lonely, cold bed.

Gideon kneeled beside the bed for his prayers, but all he could see was Augusta's face, lit up by the moon when she talked to the women at the meeting. She'd been right in everything she'd done and said but it sure stuck in his craw to admit it. Not able to keep his mind on meditation, he crawled into bed, pulled the sheet up to his neck, and let his mind go where it wanted as he stared blankly out the window at the rising moon. Not once had she told the women to be belligerent or mean to their husbands. In fact, she'd preached kindness and love. He threw his arm over his eyes. He'd go to sleep and forget about his new wife who was sweet, southern honey when she took care of his daughters and barbed wire any time she was in his presence. But all he saw in the darkness behind his eyes was one vision after another—of her helping those women; of her stretching up to hang sparkling white sheets on the line; of her wiping the sweat from her brow after she took cobblers from the oven; her stopping to hug Lucy more than a dozen times that day; and putting all four girls' hair up in rags even when the younger two didn't go to school.

Gussie heard the bed squeaking as he turned from one side to the other, thinking if he could just get comfortable for a few minutes he would quickly fall into a deep sleep. She didn't feel a bit sorry for him. He could wrestle his demons all night and not get a bit of sleep as far as she was concerned. He deserved it, the way he'd acted ever since he picked her name out of that hat.

However, her conscience was completely clear, she told herself in self-righteous indignation. She'd married him, knowing he thought she was beneath him. She'd not said a word about four little girls and all that being an instant mother entailed.

And have you practiced what you preached? that hateful voice deep inside her soul asked. *Have you flirted with your good looking husband? Have you done everything you could to make this a marriage even though it started out on the wrong foot? Be honest now, Gussie Dulan.*

"Hush," she whispered into the night air. The only answer was the loud squeak of her own bed when she flipped over to the other side to stare out at the rising moon. "The difference is those women and men want to be married to each other. They want to make a permanent home. I'm able to see what they need to do to get it. They want a family. And they're willing to work for it. I could flirt with Gideon. I could be the submissive little wife he wants even if it gagged me to death. But in the end it wouldn't bring about one bit of love from his heart. He's got his stubborn mind set on what he'll have and won't have, and I'm of the latter persuasion," she said in a whisper, hoarse with despair.

The width of one wall separated Gideon's bed, with the head board pushed up against the wall in his room, and Gussie's in the next room. It might as well have been the distance from St. Joseph, Missouri to Washington, California. Gideon wasn't going to apologize for his error in judging her on Monday morning. Gussie wasn't going to forgive him for the same.

The stalemate kept them both awake for half the night.

Chapter Five

As the last buggy pulled away from the parsonage, and Connie waved and winked at the same time, Gussie realized with a start what had just happened. Hot color filled her cheeks and her neck began to itch like it always did when she was nervous. Winnie and Bonnie had invited the twins to go home with them for supper and Gideon had given them permission to do so as long as they were home by seven. Then Connie told Lucy and Abigail about the new baby kittens she'd found hidden under her porch and asked them if they'd like to go home with her to see them.

Gussie drew her shawl tightly around her shoulders and shivered in spite of the warmth of the late afternoon sun. The women had contrived to take all Gideon's girls with them so that Gussie and Gideon could have two hours alone. None of them understood that was the worst thing they could do. Gussie and Gideon couldn't pass each other on the staircase without sparks of anger practically igniting and burning down the place. That's when the kids were around to buffer the conversation. She might need to start filling water buckets from the well in the backyard to put out the inevitable fire sure to erupt with only the preacher and the saloon dancer in the same house together.

Gideon waved at his daughters. It wasn't unusual for the

twins to go visit with Winnie and Bonnie, whose mother had died about the same time as his precious Becky. It seemed that Sam had chosen well when he picked a name from the hat because Winnie and Bonnie loved their new mother, April, sincerely. But for someone to take Lucy for a couple of hours was as rare as hen's teeth. Connie and Jack didn't know what they'd just let themselves in for, but Gideon didn't intend to question the act of kindness. The days of miracles might truly not be finished, and perhaps Lucy would be intrigued enough with the new kittens to be nice for a couple of hours.

Suddenly a prickly sensation began at the nape of Gideon's neck and inched its way slowly down his spine. Something wasn't right, yet he couldn't put his finger on it. Of course, most everything had been wrong in his life since last Monday, and every time he and Augusta were in the same room together, there was a fight. They didn't even need a big issue to lock horns over. Anything would suffice: a cup of coffee or whether the girls could spend the morning messing with bread dough on the kitchen table or counting buttons from Becky's button box. Big things could bring on something akin to an Arkansas tornado, a hurricane and an earthquake all meeting in the middle of the parlor floor. In his whole life, no one had irritated him like his new wife. He snorted loudly at that idea, then figured Augusta would ask him what was the matter with him. But she didn't say a word. Great goodness, had she fallen down dead on the porch behind him? He chanced a quick glimpse over his shoulder to find her standing beside the door, her shawl in a death grip around her shoulders, and a strange grimace on her face. Somewhat like she'd just seen a ghost. One thing for sure, he'd never seen that particular expression before.

He leaned against the porch post, watching the dust settle in the wake of Jack and Connie's wagon. A week ago the wagon train had circled up on the riverbanks. It had been the longest week of his life, yet the shortest. Augusta had taken over the household in a well-organized fashion. His girls were happier than they'd been since Becky was called home to heaven. Yes, the days went by fast, but the nights were pure agony. In the darkness he replayed every nuance, every sigh, every emotion that had been stepped on that day. Each morning he awoke with renewed intentions of telling Augusta to get out of his house; he'd pay for her room at the hotel until she could leave town. But by the time he finished breakfast in the presence of his girls who adored her, his resolve had dampened.

This morning she'd sat on the front pew of a packed church, Esther and Ruth on one side of her, Abigail on the other, and Lucy in her lap. It was the first time since he'd taken over the church in Washington that Lucy hadn't pitched at least one temper fit. After services he'd asked if there were any announcements and Augusta had stood up, faced the congregation, and announced that she and the preacher would be home from two until five during the afternoon. Anyone who wanted to come visiting was welcome. He'd bristled at her brazenness in making that announcement without consulting him first, and he told her so while they ate dinner. She'd turned surly like she always did when he tried to tone down her heathenistic ways.

The itch on his neck crept up to the top of his head. He scratched at it as the buggy carrying Lucy and Abigail disappeared around the next corner. Jack and Connie didn't live so very far away so they could bring Lucy home if she misbehaved. He turned quickly to go into the house and ran smack into Augusta, who looked absolutely as bewildered as he did.

"Excuse me," he said stiffly, jumping back like she had a case of lice and he was afraid he'd catch them.

"My fault," she said. "I should have moved, but my feet were glued to the porch." Her younger sister, Gypsy, said that the whole world stood still when Tavish held her. Well, nothing stopped running when the preacher touched her. There were no ringing bells or sparkles floating around them, either. Just further proof that this was clearly not a marriage made in the front gates of heaven, but rather in the dungeon of the other place.

"Why?" he asked.

"Don't you see, Preacher?" One side of her mouth turned up slightly. "They think they've done us a favor. We now have two whole hours of time by ourselves. Connie and Jack are so much in love that they think we'll rush right upstairs to bed."

"That's crude, Augusta," he snarled, but he did hold the door open for her. "A lady doesn't mention the bedroom or things that go on there in the presence of a gentleman."

"You're not a gentleman, Preacher. You are self-righteous and egotistical without a single shred of anything that would produce a gentleman. A Pharisee and Saducee all rolled into one if you please. And according to what you've said this past week, I'm certainly no lady. I'm a low-down saloon dancer with the morals of a well-seasoned alley cat."

"That's enough Augusta," he said bluntly right behind her.

"Shut the door while I pull the curtains," she said, easing the ribbons from the curtains and letting them fall. She'd worked hard this past week, scrubbing every day until she had everything clean for Sunday. Then yesterday she'd made ginger cookies, sugar cookies, and cinnamon cookies all day so there would be plenty for the visitors that afternoon. Next week some of the other women would be at home for Sunday afternoon visitors and they'd travel to those homes. In a month or so, it would be her turn again.

A month? Her conscience plagued her. *You're going to be here in a month?*

"Why are we doing this?" he asked.

"Because we want any one who passes to think we're doing what you say is crude," she said. "If Connie and Jack and Sam and April are good enough to take the children, we surely don't want them to think we've wasted the precious time they've given us."

Gideon blushed two shades deeper than scarlet. "You really are just a saloon girl. I'd had my moments this past week when I thought you might be changing a bit, but I see I was wrong."

"Oh, hush, Preacher, and sit down in your favorite chair over there. There's still cookies on the table, so I'll pour us some coffee and we'll prop our feet up for a couple of hours. And don't ever think I'm changing. I won't. Not for you or any other man. If I ever marry for real it will be with someone who loves me just as I am, red satin dancing dress and all."

"No decent man would have you," he snorted.

She handed him a saucer with a cup of steaming coffee in the middle, and set a platter of cookies on a table beside his chair. Pulling up her favorite rocker, she settled into it and then took off her shoes, stretching her toes. "And no woman would want you, so we're even. Maybe we should stay married just because no one else would ever want either of us," she giggled.

"Don't make fun, and there are lots of sincere God-fearing women out there in the world who would be glad to marry up with me." He picked up a cinnamon cookie and ate it in two bites.

"Name me one." She hiked up her dress tail and propped her stocking feet up on a foot stool.

"That's indecent. Cover your ankles. Women don't show men their ankles. It's not right," he said, his voice a bit hoarse from desire romping through his veins. He'd have to work harder at not letting this loose woman influence his thinking, he figured as he shoved more cookie into his mouth. She wasn't playing one bit fair, displaying her ankles like that. However, every man in town had seen them on the day he married her. That short-tailed red dress had barely come to the top of her shoes, showing off a healthy dose of black stockings. Indecent. Just like he'd said.

"You're not just a man. You are my husband, Preacher. And I suppose when it's all said and done, no one would ever believe we spent the evening hours in a house alone with us across the room from each other," she smiled.

He rolled his eyes. There was no changing a leopard's spots or a coarse saloon girl's thinking either.

"Tell me, Preacher, what brought you out here? You must have had a church somewhere? Did you leave it before or after the twins were born?" She asked.

"Why are you asking?" He raised an eyebrow.

"We got two hours. It's Sunday. I reckon you'd have a fit if I drug out my sewing or crocheting. If I used the two hours to scrub down the stairs, you'd probably fall down on your knees and beg God to send a legion of demons to haul my sorry carcass straight to hell. I just thought we'd make some conversation, Preacher. Is that so hard to understand? I promise if you tell me your story I won't feel sorry for you and change my mind about you sleeping with me," she said.

"I wouldn't dishonor my sweet Becky's memory!" He was totally aghast.

"I'm sure of it," she said. "But you would have already dishonored it had I been standing there in my faded calico dress or my blue traveling suit. It was the red dress that put you off, honey. Admit it. You wanted a wife. You just didn't want one who'd wear a fancy dress like that."

"It was after the twins were born, before Abigail and Lucy were born," he said, throwing up his hands in defeat. "And don't you mention Becky's name again. You aren't fit to even think the name of someone as pure as she was."

"Evidently she wasn't that pure. Unless those girls were born by immaculate conception," Gussie said.

"That is enough! I won't have that kind of vulgarity in my presence," he shouted.

"Temper, temper," Gussie said. "I'll just go up to my room and have a rest. It's plain as the snout on a sow that we can't carry on a conversation. Strange, Jesus was able to talk to Mary Magdalene and look what she'd been, and he had no trouble with the woman at the well, and she'd had how many husbands? Seven wasn't it? But you're so righteous and full of yourself that you can't even answer a few questions without getting your back up in hackles."

"Sit down, Augusta," he said, his tone softening so that she did what he said. "You are right. I shouldn't have judged you, but I'm still not going to stay married to you. I'm not sure how we'll take care of this mistake. Seems the only thing to do is for one of us to leave Washington. I have my church here and I like it. I wouldn't want you to stay if you're going to go down the street and work in a saloon. It would be the ruin of my reputation and my church. So I suppose you should leave. A stage will be stopping at the general store tomorrow morning at ten. I guess you should be on it."

Her heart turned into a solid lump of blackened coal in her chest. Burned to a crisp. So hard it could never fall in love. He was dismissing her and she would never see those precious little girls again. "I guess it would be best," she whispered.

"Now, we've still got the better part of two hours, Augusta," he said. "I'll tell you about my sweet Becky. That's her on the mantle there. A lovely lady. Born and raised by the preacher in the adjoining town where I grew up. Becky Witherton, she was, and I fell in love with her the first time I saw her at a tent revival. Her father was preaching and her mother led the singing. We were seventeen. I gave my heart and life to God in that revival and the next year I was given my first country church to pastor. The year after that we were married. She'd been raised in a fine Christian home and our lives required very little adjustments when we were married. She moved from one parsonage to the other. Two years after that the twins were born. When they were a year old I felt the Lord calling me to the frontier to bring the gospel to the miners. I sold our farm, quit the church, and told Becky about my decision."

"After you sold your farm and quit the church? You just walked in one day and said, 'Hey darlin', pack up the wagon here we're going to California'? You were wrong when you said she was a sweet woman. She was either stone stupid or a lily white saint. You didn't even ask her?" Gussie was amazed.

"No, it is the man's place to make a living wherever God sends him. It was Becky's place to go whither I should go. Like Ruth did in the Bible," Gideon reminded her.

Gussie just shook her head in astonishment.

"Do you want me to go on or will you go on upstairs and take an afternoon rest?" he asked bluntly.

"Oh, continue, by all means. I'm beginning to see the picture a little clearer. Tell me though, what would you do if someone pulled a like stunt on one of your daughters? Would you just sit still and tell them to go with their husbands? Take their two little baby girls and leave everything they ever had or knew behind them?"

"Of course," he said, then felt the sharp prick of a blatant lie to his heart. He'd fight any man who drug his daughters halfway across the world to pan for gold and preach in a brush arbor or out in the open. He'd never considered what he'd asked Becky to do. That she'd done it without a cross word elevated her to absolute sainthood right then and there. Gideon Jefferson didn't need another wife. Not now. Not ever. He'd already had one who could never be replaced.

"Do go on," Gussie said. No wonder he thought he could boss her around like she was a child. He'd been spoiled to that kind of lily-livered woman.

"We went to St. Joseph, Missouri and traveled with a wagon train of young folks looking for a better life in California. Gold miners. It was an adventure. By the time we reached our stake Becky was expecting Abigail. She was born one rainy night. There were no doctors amongst us or anywhere near but a fine lady whose husband's claim was next to ours helped her through the difficult birth. We didn't get rich overnight, but slowly the gold began to mount up and before long we had enough to build a small cabin."

"What did you live in before that?" Gussie asked.

"The wagon for a while, then a brush hut," Gideon said. "But Becky didn't complain. She took care of the children, cooked our food and was a good wife."

"I bet she was," Gussie set her jaw, thinking of a woman giving birth with only the lady from the next camp to help her. Becky was probably sitting in heaven with a crown so heavy with jewels that it was breaking her neck.

"Two years later we had almost enough to build a little church, but she took sick after Lucy was born. Fevers. Never could figure out what was causing them. Didn't seem to be contagious because no one else got it. She had this little sling she kept Lucy in, tied up around her shoulders, while she helped me pan for gold on the days when the fever didn't put her to bed," he said, misty-eyed at the memory.

"She panned for gold, too?" Gussie asked, incredulously.

"Oh, yes. We all did. Even had little bitty pans for the twins. She died when Lucy was three months old. About that time Hank and Jake brought out a wagon train load of others who had the gold itch. I sold one of them eighty percent of my claim. Then the men who'd come without wives got this idea that we could send Hank and Jake back east for a load of wives. If they could bring gold miners, they could bring wives. You know the rest," he said.

"So did you get rich?" She asked.

"I didn't come out here to get rich. I came to bring God's gospel to the miners," he said heavily.

"Did you get rich, though?" She asked.

"Yes, I did. And in doing so I lost Becky," he said.

"And it didn't teach you one iota about women, did it Preacher? Well, I'm going upstairs to pack. If I'm leaving tomorrow there's things I need to do and I'd rather the girls didn't see me doing it," she said.

"It's for the best," he agreed. After Becky's death, he'd begun to wonder if he'd really heard God's voice to his own soul telling him to go to California to preach or if he'd been listening to his own heart telling him he wanted an adventure. Now he wondered again if he'd been paying attention to what he wanted when he handed over his share of gold for Hank and Jake to bring him a wife. If it had been the Heavenly Father's will, he surely would not have picked Augusta Dulan's name from the hat.

"Dulan, the same as Jake's name," he mumbled. "That's a bit strange."

He pondered over the fact until it became an obsession. Surely she wasn't related to Jake Dulan. Couldn't be. Jake was a man's man; he would have never put up with one of his daughters dancing in a saloon. Not any more than Gideon would stand by and let one of his daughters do the same. Finally he wandered up the stairs, only to find Augusta's bedroom door open as she repacked her trunk.

"Are you related to Jake Dulan? And why didn't he make the trip back with Hank?" he asked, ignoring the catch in the pit of his stomach at the idea of her leaving. Saying it wasn't so hard. Accepting it for the best was pretty easy. But to watch her fold her day dresses was another matter. No more hot breakfast or curls bouncing in Esther and Ruth's hair as they skipped happily down the road to school. Had he been too rash in sending her away? Perhaps she could stay on as a housekeeper just until he could find a real wife?

Now wouldn't that be horrid? Augusta in the house while he courted another woman, yet was married on paper to Augusta. What a mess he'd made out of his life that morning when he gave in to his daughter's screaming tantrum and married the woman. It was all Lucy's fault when the facts were in, he decided.

"Jake died in St. Joseph. I am the oldest of five girls he produced in his lifetime of marriages," she said. "Now if you'll excuse me—" She slammed the door in his face.

There was no way she was going to fold her unmentionables in front of the preacher. Not even if they had vowed to love each other.

His curiosity piqued, his pride wounded, he went back down the stairs. He sat in his chair, trying to make sense of the topsy-turvy emotions creating devastation so deep inside him that it ached. Thank goodness it would be all over by just after lunch tomorrow. There were lots of women in town now and Gideon wasn't a poor man. He could afford to pay any one of them to help him out with the household chores and keeping the children. He'd start by asking Connie if she would be interested in keeping the younger two girls in the day time. Even if he couldn't roll their hair every night, he could at least prepare their supper and get them to bed, especially with Esther and Ruth's help. Things would settle into a new routine.

Oh but he dreaded the fit Lucy was going to throw.

Chapter Six

Dark rings circled Gideon's deep brown eyes and he avoided any direct eye contact with Augusta that morning. The night before had been the worst he'd ever spent. Not even when Becky labored through two nights with Lucy had he felt so wrung out when it was over. He shoveled sausage gravy and biscuits into his mouth, not tasting one morsel of the well-prepared breakfast.

"I've got several errands to run this morning. I shall return by lunch time," he said when he'd finished the last of his coffee.

"You'll be here by one, I assume?" Gussie raised an eyebrow. Her trunk was repacked and ready to be hauled to the stagecoach. Her own eyes were red and swollen from crying all night. Not that she'd shed one single tear for the pompous preacher, but rather for the four little girls still having breakfast. She'd known in her young life what it was to be without a mother and leaving these four who'd stolen her heart would be the most difficult thing she'd ever been required to do. She'd worried about how to tell them good-bye all night, and still didn't have a clue as to how to go about it.

"Of course, I will be back by dinner time. I guess you'll be getting the washing done this morning, since it is Monday?" He asked stiffly.

"It will be on the line by the time you return," she told him. Actually, doing the laundry would give her something to do all morning. It would keep her mind off the horrendous job of at least telling Abigail and Lucy she was leaving. The older two girls would simply have to find out when they came home from school that evening. She hoped all four of them kept the preacher up all night with their howling. Especially Lucy. If only she could take Lucy with her. Poor little thing had only known her mother's love for a few months. No wonder her temper was so volatile.

Gideon slipped on his frock coat, set his hat at just the right angle and was out the front door before she could say anything else. He made up his mind not to return until fifteen minutes before the stagecoach was due to leave. That way he'd have to rush to get her trunk down the steps and out the door. He'd put her on the coach and it would be gone before he could do anything rash, like letting his lust overtake his good sense. *Father,* he prayed earnestly on the way to the livery, *please get this woman out of my life. I made a terrible mistake when I sent for a wife. I should have waited for you to bring one to me, if it was your will. Nevertheless, as our dear Jesus prayed, not my will but thine. I shall forever be thy servant. Please hear my prayer. Amen.*

He intended to ride out to the mines, spend the morning visiting amongst the miners, see his old acquaintances, renew ties, and invite them all to church as he did so. Ralph, the owner of the livery harnessed up Gideon's horse to his buggy and handed him the reins, telling him to be careful. He said his arm which had been broken in a mining accident was paining him awful that morning and it meant cold rain was in the forecast. Gideon smiled at the elderly man and patted him on the shoulder. Broken bones didn't tell one thing about weather. That was an old wive's tale.

Gussie took the rag rollers from Esther and Ruth's hair, pulled the sides and part of the top back to tie with a ribbon, kissed them each several times, and watched until they were out of sight. She brushed away a steady stream of tears, being careful not to let Abigail or Lucy see.

"Okay, ladies, let's get your rollers out and get your shoes on. We've got a washing to do before dinner time. What do you say we make something special for dinner today?" She said, squatting down to hold them both in a tight hug.

Lucy squealed and giggled. "Breaking me bones, Momma."

Gussie had to swallow several times to get the lump down her throat. *Momma.* Would she ever have her own daughters to call her that? She doubted it. Like the preacher said, no man wanted a wife who'd danced before men in a saloon. Reluctantly, she let them and her heart go at the same time.

The clotheslines were filled with clean clothing and sheets by midmorning. She stirred up two batches of sugar cookies, letting Abigail and Lucy cut them into shapes while she drank in the sight of them every moment she could. Abigail with her light brown hair and perfectly round little face, so serious about her job. Lucy, a nightmare on wheels, full of giggles, eating as much of the dough as she cut into shapes. She'd never forget the week she had four precious daughters even if she did have to contend with one grouchy husband to get them.

At straight up twelve o'clock she had a pot roast ready. The aroma of freshly baked loaves of sourdough bread filled the entire house. The preacher should have been home by now. He was very adamant about meals being on time every day even if he never once had a kind, or otherwise, word to say about her food. At a quarter past twelve she set Abigail and Lucy up the table and the three of them had dinner. The preacher could make his own meal after she was gone and she hoped it had grown so cold it gagged him. She sent the children to their room for their afternoon nap, and followed them upstairs to change into her dark blue traveling dress. In a couple of weeks she'd be at Garnet's place in Frenchman's Ford, Nevada. Garnet had left the wagon train and had gone to town that night with intentions of finding a job playing a piano for a saloon. If she had, perhaps she could help Gussie find a job dancing in the same place. Suddenly, all the red satin dresses and men screaming her name from the saloon floors didn't appeal to her. She'd trade it all for the four little girls she'd inherited. Matter of fact, she'd give it all back just for Lucy. But the option wasn't hers to have. She'd be gone in less than an hour. As soon as the preacher arrived to carry her trunk to the general store.

She heard the stage rumble down the street outside the parsonage. The emptiness in her heart and the silence in the house was so loud she could hardly bear it. She dressed quickly and eased the door open to Abigail and Lucy's room. Lucy snuggled up to Abigail's back with one arm slung around her older sister. Would Willow and Gypsy have looked like that when they'd been little girls if they'd known each other? Would she and Garnet have ever been that close had they been given the privilege of knowing the other existed all those years? She liked to think so.

The big clock in the foyer downstairs struck one o'clock. The preacher would be in an unholy rush when he came tearing in the house. He was most likely running late and at that very moment at the store, telling the stagecoach to wait until he could get his wife from the parsonage. She smiled but it didn't reach her eyes.

In the spring of the year when she agreed to join the wagon train with her four sisters, she'd doubted her own instincts toward motherhood, and now after only a week of playing the game, it was tearing her heart out to leave it behind. She'd only thought she'd known heartbreak before; had never felt her heart break into a million pieces and could do nothing to stop the hurt. She had never realized that something so small and irritable as a two-year-old could affect her life so much. She had never known that she would enjoy hearing herself referred to as Momma so much. She'd never known the warmth, the love or the joy of just being needed. Gussie could wring the preacher's neck for giving her that and then taking it from her all within seven days. He could have offered to let her stay on as a governess and housekeeper. Just that much until they were grown. But oh, no, the rat had just blandly told her it was time for her to go now; now that her soul was wrapped around the girls and crying out with the pain. Had Gussie's own mother felt like that in those few moments she had before she died right after Gussie was born? Had her soul begged for a few more minutes to cradle her only child in her arms before she was whisked into eternity?

Gussie tip-toed to the edge of the bed and very carefully planted a kiss on each of their foreheads. "Good-bye my sweet daughters. I will keep you forever in my heart," she said.

She sat down on the stair steps to wait. She shut her eyes tightly for a few minutes and was surprised that it was dark when she opened them. A check out the front window let her know there was a storm brewing, coming in from the north. It had blotted out the sun already, and seemed to be poetic justice. Her mood was every bit as dark as it was outside. A zagged bolt of lightning shot through the sky. *Too late,* she thought. *My heart is already broken.* The thunder that followed it rattled the walls and Becky's picture fell from the mantle onto the floor. Gussie picked it up and set it back on the mantle. At least the glass hadn't broken. The preacher would blame her for sure, had it been. Truth was, she didn't want to take the woman's place. She just wanted to enjoy the daughters she'd left behind. If Becky could jerk Gideon up to heaven with her, they could both spend eternity together and Gussie would be satisfied to raise the girls.

There was no sweet raindrops to herald the upcoming torrent. It just started from nothing, one moment a stillness following the sharp crack of thunder, the next a downpour that obliterated the church next door from her view. That's all she needed, she thought as she folded her arms over her chest. She'd be soaked just getting from the store to the stage. One thing for sure the stage wasn't going anywhere until the weather calmed down a bit. Even well-trained horses were skittish in a thunderstorm. There was no way she was going to miss that stage now.

Gideon enjoyed the ride out to the mines and panning operations. Times had been few and far between when he went anywhere without children tagging along. It was part of being a father and he embraced his responsibilities with no self-pity, but it was nice to drive along in the silence of the stimulating morning air without having to worry with two to four little girls in the buggy with him.

If only he could erase that last vision of Augusta in the kitchen he would be the most content man on the face of the earth. But there she was in that faded gingham checked dress, her hair tied back with a blue ribbon, the blonde and brown mixture flowing down past her waist. The word "strange" came to mind as he mindlessly let the horse have a little more rein. Strange colored hair; not brown, yet not blonde either. A mixture of both that brightened in the sunlight. He'd peeked out the kitchen window one morning for a long time, just keeping an eye on his wife. The sun had danced on the blonde streaks in her hair, and she'd appeared to be so happy with the girls, encouraging them to count the blossoms on the bougainvillea creeping up the back porch post. In just a week Lucy could make it all the way to twenty. And Abigail had simply flourished this week. She had mastered counting all the way to a hundred.

Thinking of the strange color of her hair brought him to the even odder color of her eyes. Not green by any means, they just missed blue by a shade or two. They were big and round, set behind heavy dark lashes and under perfectly arched eyebrows which matched the darker shade of her hair. Jake Dulan had eyes like that only his didn't seem like they could see straight into a man's soul like Augusta's did.

Gideon smelled the rich aroma of coffee long before he reached the camp sites. He missed it all: the biting morning air, the thrill of the search, the taste of coffee the first thing in the morning. But the Lord had been good to Gideon Jefferson. He'd let him find enough gold nuggets to make him a rich man, and now Gideon must follow his calling and preach the gospel to lost souls, all the while taking care of the flock that had been put into his care right there in Washington.

He stopped at one camp after another, having coffee, eating a chunk of hoe cake with one family. Inviting them all to church. Asking about their well being. Answering questions about the new brides who'd arrived. He even smiled when he told about his new wife, Augusta, and how much the girls loved her. Well, it wasn't an outright lie. They did love her and he had no doubt that she loved them. He simply committed the sin of omission by not telling the good people that he simply could not abide the woman and that she literally hated him with a passion.

In the middle of the morning he checked his pocket watch. Ten-thirty. He was two hours from Washington. Timing was perfect. He'd get back into town at just the right time to hurriedly take her to the stage, wave good-bye, and then drag Lucy home by the arm while she screamed and kicked. He bid everyone a good week and waved without even looking to the north at the solid bank of storm clouds rolling in like black smoke. He whistled as he slapped the reins against the horse's flanks. The day had gone just like he'd planned.

At noon his stomach rumbled at the same time the first flash of lightning crackled in the sky. It was followed by a clap of thunder that jerked Gideon's attention from a memory of Augusta in that red dress, looking like the kind of woman she apparently really was. So Ralph, the livery owner, had been right after all. That didn't mean it was his bones telling him the weather was going to be wet. It just meant his bones hurt and the weather got bad. Surely his bones ached when the weather didn't get bad. Gideon turned the collar of his overcoat up, ducked his head against the oncoming wind, and held on to his hat as he urged the horse into a trot. Thirty more minutes and he'd send Augusta on her way. It didn't matter if she was wet down to her unmentionables. Maybe she'd catch pneumonia and die before she reached her sister's place and he wouldn't have to file for a bill of divorcement. As if in retaliation for such an unkind spirit, the wind picked up, the rain peppered against him in cold bullets, and lightning bolts struck a tree off to one side of the road, splitting it in half.

"Okay, okay," he shouted. "I'm sorry."

Not as sorry as he was when the back wheel of the buggy fell off when it hit a rock. One moment he was sitting on the wagon seat. Wet, yes, but moving ahead. The next he was thrown out into the muddy road, face down in a puddle. He braced up on his elbows, took stock of what had happened, and watched his hat blow somewhere down toward the southern part of the state. There was nothing to do but fix the wheel—in the rain and mud, water pouring into his eyes and down his back. At least the horse hadn't been spooked and stampeded.

It took the better part of an hour. When he checked his watch it was almost two o'clock. Augusta would be gone by the time he arrived. Maybe God had been working for him after all instead of against him. He wouldn't have to watch her leave now. She would have left the girls with Connie, no doubt. By the time he reached home, Connie would have already taken care of the first onslaught of tantrums from Lucy and dried Abigail's tears. He'd have to deal with the twins about the same time he got home, but he could do that much, if Connie would just take care of Lucy.

The going was very slow with the makeshift job he'd done on the wheel, but he arrived home in the middle of the afternoon. There was no stage in front of the store, so that problem had taken care of itself. He and Ralph spent ten minutes discussing the wheel, and Ralph assured him that he'd rub the horse down and give him extra oats that evening. Then Gideon dragged his sodden body down the street to face a house as empty as his heart.

"Daddy, daddy, guess what we made for supper?" Lucy met him at the door. "We made a peach cobbler. We founded peaches in the closet and I got to roll out the pie dough."

"That's good. Daddy has got to go upstairs now and change his wet clothes. Tell Connie that I'll be down shortly and she can go home," Gideon said.

"Why would Connie be here?" Gussie asked from the doorway to the kitchen. "And just why weren't you here when you were supposed to be? I missed it, you know."

"Why are you here?" Gideon turned on her like a cornered cougar. "Didn't you have enough sense to get someone to come in and watch the kids until I could get home? Are you so stupid to think that . . ."

Her finger stopped him. It was a fraction of an inch from his flaring, wet nostrils. "Don't you dare talk to me like that in front of the kids," she hissed. "We'll discuss this in the study as soon as you are dry. I wouldn't care if you died of pneumonia if you'd do it fast and I wouldn't have to see to you, but it sure upsets me for you to stand there dripping on my clean rug."

"You meet me in the study in ten minutes, woman," he said.

"Don't you call me *woman*. I have a name," she called after him. "And don't you be late again, Preacher. Ten minutes. On the eleventh minute I'll march down the street and find another job."

He tore at his wet clothing so fast that he ripped two buttons from his shirt. One popped all the way across the room and slid under the bed. The other one skidded off the wall and rolled under the wardrobe. How dare that woman threaten him!

What makes you so sure she's threatening you? A voice that sounded almost like Becky's said in low tones. *She's right you know? You've been a complete stubborn mule ever since her wedding day. You ain't no prize, Gideon Jefferson. You are opinionated and mean-spirited some of the time. Wake up and face the music.*

Gussie stood by the door, tapping her foot and glaring at the clock when Gideon appeared at the top of the stairs in nine minutes and thirty seconds. His vest was unbuttoned, hair sported whole raindrops on the top, and he was barefoot. If she wanted a full-fledged fight, then he'd bring her one. She should have had the sense to leave when she had the chance. And that wasn't Becky's voice talking to him. She'd never say ugly things like that; not his precious Becky.

"The girls are stringing buttons," she nodded toward the kitchen. "After you, Preacher." She waited beside the opened study door.

"Ladies first," he said acidly.

"Then you should for sure go first," she said with just as much cutting edge to her voice as he had. "After all, in your own words, I'm not a lady."

He marched in ahead of her and sat down in his chair behind his desk, hoping his very presence and hateful glower would intimidate her.

It didn't.

She braced her hands on the desk and leaned over it. "Now where have you been? Even in the storm you had time to get here. The stage didn't leave the store until two o'clock straight up."

"Why weren't you on it?" He asked.

"And leave the girls alone in this house with a storm raging outside? Leave it to an ignorant man to think a four-year-old and a two-year-old wouldn't be scared out of their wits in a bad storm like that, even with an adult here. You

would have had me leave them alone? Some father you
are," Gussie said as she gritted her teeth.

"Don't you dare tell me what kind of father I am. I did
fine raising my children before you came on the scene and
I'll do fine again." He leaned forward until they were nose
to nose again. For just a second, it flashed through his mind
that he could easily kiss her from that point. What would
it be like to taste those lips? To take all those pins from
her hair and tangle it up in his hands?

"I'm sure you will. They'll be hoydens with no manners
or social graces because you are so wound up in yourself,
you can't see the forest for the trees," she said.

"What's that supposed to mean?" Gideon asked. *Just one
kiss,* his heart begged, but his mind said that he'd get a
black eye for his efforts.

"It means you stayed too long out there doing whatever
it is you were doing. It means you should have watched
the sky a little better. It means you aren't responsible. It
means that I wouldn't have left those babies by themselves
even if I do have to live with you for another week before
the next stage comes through," she said.

Gideon paled. The grimace in his face wasn't anything
like a smile. Her eyes widened as she realized what she'd
just said and the effect it had on him.

"There is another train next Monday isn't there? You
said it came once a week," she whispered, the wind suddenly gone from the sails of anger.

"It does," he said weakly. "It comes through here once
a week going most anywhere in these parts. But it doesn't
go back east until the passes are passable. Augusta, that
was the last stage coming in or going out of Washington
in that direction until the spring thaw; sometime toward the
end of March. That's why Hank pushed you all so hard to
get here before the passes were snowed in. He and Annie
probably barely made it through. I heard last week they
were pushing it to get one more stage out. There sure won't
be another one before spring. The new Pony Express might

be able to get through with mail, but unless you want to ride on the back of a fast moving horse and carry the mail, you are here until the spring thaw."

She grinned, then giggled. Then one of those big guffaws exploded, bouncing around the room like the sparks when they fought. Four months? She'd be stark-raving mad living in the same house with the preacher that long. She'd be seeing spiders on the ceiling and standing on her head in hot ashes.

"What's so funny?" he asked forlornly. "I don't see one thing humorous about the situation." His crazy heart was doing some kind of excited flip-flops at keeping Augusta for a few months. Didn't it know that within five months one of them would kill the other? No house was big enough to contain a preacher and a saloon girl. No, he'd go further than that. The state of California wasn't big enough for both of them, not even for five months.

Gussie wiped her eyes on the tail of her apron. Her heart was singing some song about being able to spend five months with the girls. She reminded it that the price she'd pay for those months was almighty steep.

"Heaven help us," she said between hiccups as she marched out of the study.

"Heaven ain't even that powerful," Gideon mumbled.

Chapter Seven

Gussie buttoned the front of Lucy's cape. Two days of rain had kept the ground wet and black clouds on the horizon threatened more sometime in the night. She just hoped the girls didn't get their feet too wet. She'd be sure to heat bricks to slip in the foot of their beds after the meeting, but she wasn't missing her Tuesday night gathering with the other women. Looking forward to that half hour was what had kept her from yanking every strand of the preacher's hair out all day long. Just being in the presence of the other brides and hearing their problems helped all of them keep their own trials in the proper perspective.

"Daddy, we're going now. We'll be the first ones there," Esther called through the open door of the study.

"I think you will." Gideon put aside his paper and went to the door. "But then you've got less distance to cover and it is ten minutes until time for the meeting. Oh, Augusta, I have posted a message at the store, and asked Connie when I was out and about this morning, to put out the word that your meeting will be held in the church from now on. Tuesday nights at six. Weather is getting too unpredictable for you ladies to be standing out in the cold and wet, and something tells me you'd still have these meetings even if you had to stand in freezing rain."

Gussie was shocked speechless. Had the preacher actually done something nice for her and the other brides? She nodded curtly and picked up Lucy to carry her across the lawn to the church right next door. The windows were yellow with lights already lit and waiting. She should have expressed her thanks, but the preacher saying something in a tone that wasn't whitewashed with rage made her feel like she was waking from a dream, experiencing that moment when reality and dreams were one.

She and the little girls took a seat on the front pew and waited. Not for long though, as the other women filtered in quickly, taking seats and whispering amongst themselves quietly. Gussie wondered if she should take control of the meeting or if Connie would step up for the first words again. She wasn't so sure she could find a voice to say a word.

The dilemma was solved when the back door swung open and Gideon marched down the center aisle. Silence so heavy it seemed to drip from the rafters followed him to the pulpit. Men weren't a part of their meetings, not in the physical sense anyway. The whole purpose of their time together would be in vain if the men were allowed to join the meetings.

"Ladies, I assure you I'm only here for a moment," he said with a smile, hoping to cut through the tension. "I want you to feel free to use this building for your meetings every week. I've penciled in Tuesday nights at this time so no one else will have use of the church. Since you are going to be a ladies-only organization, I have decided to call you the Ladies' Auxiliary. While you have your meeting on Tuesday nights, the men will have a meeting in my home or on the grounds if the weather permits. After half an hour for each of us to take care of our business, it is my proposal that we men then join you women for a half hour social. Tonight I will bring the refreshments. Augusta made enough cookies on Sunday to feed an army of hungry soldiers and there was plenty leftover. Next week each of you can bring a dessert of some kind and we'll provide drinks since we live next door and it will be easy for us to do so. Now I will leave you to your Auxiliary meeting."

Let Augusta chew on that for a while, Gideon thought. She'd invited anyone who wanted to visit to come around last Sunday and hadn't asked for his opinion on the matter. Maybe he'd planned a trip out to the miners that afternoon for a late afternoon service for those who couldn't come to town for church. Not that he had, but she sure hadn't asked before she committed him to an afternoon at home. So he could well get in the middle of her plans without saying a word to her. Besides, he was the man of the house and he intended to stay that way.

Gussie thought about tearing a nice long length of fabric from the tail of her petticoat and tying it firmly around his neck. Seeing his face turn blue and his eyes pop out of their sockets might be enough revenge for his arrogance. She liked meeting outside in the place where they'd circled their wagons the last time. They didn't need some fancy name and they sure didn't need to have a social afterwards.

"Thank you," Connie said as he left the pulpit. "Shall we come to your house or will your bring the men and refreshments to the church?"

"We'll wait for you and Augusta to come and fetch the cookies and us men folks in a half an hour," he said as he shut the doors behind him.

"I'm not so sure I like it," Connie said, taking the preacher's place behind the pulpit. "Seems like we ought to be in the circle."

"It's time to move on now," Berdie said. "We're not on the wagon train any more. We're married women. Part of a town and community. It's time for us to give up the wagons, and I don't mean just physically."

"Like a baby giving up their tag-along blanket," Viola said as she laughed from the back of the church. "It's time for us to grow up. Is that what you're saying, Berdie?"

"That's what I'm saying. Now let's get on with the business. Connie's lessons helped bring about the results I wanted, but I like flirting so much more than I thought I would that I wondered if I could go back for some more lessons?" Berdie said.

"Sure," Connie said. "Jack is usually out all afternoon. Wednesdays are a good time for me to sit and visit. Anyone who wants to join me and Berdie is welcome. Bring your mending."

"And I've got a problem with those two boys I inherited," another lady said from the front pew. "Gussie, is Wednesday a good day for us to talk about children. I'll have to bring the little one. He's a handful."

"Ain't none of them ever going to be worse than Lucy, so bring him on. Bring your mending. Maybe it won't rain and we can sit in the backyard and the children can play," Gussie said.

"How about this name the preacher has given us?" Connie said. "Are we in agreement to let it stand like that? What do you think Gussie? You've been our backbone through this trip."

"Thank you," Gussie said from her place on the front pew. "Never thought I'd hear you say that, though."

"Wouldn't have if I hadn't been so blasted scared of Jack. Lord, all I could think that whole night when I huddled in the rocking chair with a blanket around me, my clothes and shoes all still on, was that if I could just talk to Gussie, she'd tell me what to do," Connie said. "Now how about this fancy-shmancy name?"

"A name don't make or break nothing," Viola said, brushing back a long strand of strawberry-blonde hair from her cheeks. "Preacher Gideon can call us the Women's Circle for all I care. Long as we got a place to have a little meeting so we can set up the rest of the week."

Gussie nodded. The preacher had thought he was putting one over on her. That smug look on his face when he stood behind the pulpit said that he was in charge and there was nothing she could do about it. Well, never underestimate the powers of a Dulan woman. He was waiting for a fight when the social was over; she'd give him one. But when she got finished he sure wouldn't be the victor and his mind would be in a spin worse than a Tennessee whirlwind.

Stories were exchanged for the rest of the meeting and then it was time for Gussie and Connie to traipse across the connecting lawns to the parsonage where the men waited in knots in the front yard, on the porch, in the living room, kitchen, and study. Gussie heard talk of cows, gold, pigs, crops, and war as she passed one group after another. What would Gideon do if the South did secede from the United States of America? He'd been raised in the South just like she had been, but he was a Californian now. Where would he stand? Talk had it that the South would split away within the next six months. Could it be he'd go off to fight and she could stay right there and raise the girls?

With a wink and a little flirty sashaying, Connie had Jack and two other husbands carrying the cookie tins back to the church. Berdie and Viola had set up a table of sorts, with intentions of bringing a tablecloth and a bucket for the punch next week. Viola declared she was ordering a real glass punch bowl before long. After all, there would be other occasions when it would be needed.

When the last of the couples disappeared in the first sprinkles of still more rain, Gideon blew out all the lamps and shut the doors, only to find Augusta playing a game with his four daughters. It was hard to tell which one was giggling hardest, Augusta or Lucy, as they all five chased around catching raindrops on their tongues.

"I got one," Augusta announced. "Mmmmm, it tastes like peppermint."

"Me, too." Lucy stopped, her little face skewing up in deep thought. "It just tastes like water to me."

"Lucy, you're s'posed to use your 'magination," Esther said, sticking her own tongue out as far as it would go. "I got one, I did. And it tastes just like, just like, hmmm, it tastes like cinnamon sugar cookies."

"Stop this nonsense," Gideon yelled from the porch steps. "Get in the house right now."

"Would you be talking to me in that tone of voice?" Gussie asked so softly, it scared him.

"I'm talking to all of you. Running around acting like a bunch of fools," he said, grabbing Augusta by the arm, fully well expecting her to follow his lead toward the house.

She jerked her arm free and glared at him. "Don't you touch me. Don't you ever touch me again, not when you are treating me like a child."

"You are my wife. I can touch you if I want and there's not a thing you can do about it. Go on in the house, girls. Augusta and I will be in in a moment," he said. All four girls ran toward the porch. All four of them with their tongues out, trying to catch just one more raindrop before they went inside.

"You are my wife," he stated again. "That means I can do whatever I like and there's not a court in the nation that would say a word. You might as well wake up and realize you don't have any rights, Augusta. Other than the right to a roof over your head which you will have to keep clean, and food on the table which you will prepare."

Gussie stuck out her tongue, catching more than one drop on the end of it. "Yep, peppermint. Come on Preacher. We're getting wet out here," she looped her arm through his and led the way.

Hadn't she heard a word he said? Was she daft or just playing dumb?

Gussie was amazed at the warmth down deep in the pits of her stomach. She had four months to retrain this man. Creating a decent, loving husband from the south end of a north bound Missouri mule wasn't going to be an easy feat, but she could do it. She had every confidence as they walked up on the porch, arm in arm like two newlyweds.

Not that she wanted him. Not on a bet. But at least she'd leave him a little better person for the next woman, who she hoped wasn't some mealy-mouthed, trained puppy.

That was easy enough, Gideon figured as he strolled the few yards from the church lawn to the front porch of the parsonage. If he'd known that she needed it put into simple words that she could understand, he would have done so from the beginning. Now that they were on the right footing, he'd remind her often of her so-called rights, letting her know that she wasn't anything but a common saloon girl. Oh, he wasn't going to keep the tramp, but he might train her in the ways of a real wife so that someday when some blind, ignorant fool came along and thought himself in love, she would at least know her place.

When they reached the top step her feet slipped and she fell backwards down the steps, pulling the preacher right along with her. It all happened in less time than it takes a mosquito to blink. She had been about to let go of his arm so he could stand aside like the gentleman he thought himself to be and let her enter before him, when suddenly her wet shoes lost traction on the slick step. She landed with a plop, knocking the wind out of her lungs, then another thud and he was on top of her, his big muscular body stretched out like a blanket, covering her, his eyes wide open and his mouth so close it made her crosseyed to look at it.

Just as suddenly that mouth closed over hers and the lightning zipping across the dark skies was nothing compared to the fireworks display which lit up her heart. That's the way a kiss was supposed to be. That's what Willow and Gypsy were talking about when they said they were leaving the train to go find Rafe and Tavish. Now she understood. Kisses she'd shared with other men didn't compare. From now on she'd look for a man who could kiss like that. But it wouldn't be the almighty preacher Gideon Jefferson.

Gideon tasted rain blended with cinnamon sugar cookies on her lips. Heaven opened up, the presence of which made his heart glow with happiness. Never had he felt so alive. So he hadn't buried his heart with Becky after all. He could still feel passion. Now he knew he could marry again. But it would never be with a woman like Augusta Dulan. Not a saloon girl.

"Well," she huffed as he clumsily pushed himself off her and sat down with a clunk on the bottom step. "Are you injured?"

"No, are you?" He asked, his voice raspy.

"No, just my pride," she said, touching her mouth to see if it was as hot as it felt.

"You have pride?" he asked bluntly.

She jumped up and stormed into the house. Living with that man was going to be trial enough for the next few months. If she hadn't killed him graveyard-dead by spring, then she fully well deserved to find another man. Forget about training him for wife number three. Anyone stupid enough to marry him could do their own dirty work. Or else be no more than a southern slave with no rights.

"Momma, I brought down the rollers," Esther held up a basket of rags cut to the right size to do their hair. "Your face is all red. Momma are you all right?"

"I'm fine," Gussie said. "Just fine. Let's get busy making you all four beautiful for tomorrow." She left the door wide open and hoped the preacher caught his death out there on the porch. "You first tonight; Ruth, next. Then while you two get ready for bed, I'll take care of Abigail and Lucy."

Gideon sat on the porch a while longer, calming his racing heart, stilling his sinful thoughts, and counting just how many days would have to pass before he'd be rid of that sassy piece of baggage he'd been forced to marry. Finally he went inside to find Augusta putting the last rag in Lucy's hair. Why she bothered doing Abigail and Lucy's hair every night was a mystery to him. Most days the two children didn't go anywhere or see anyone except him and Augusta. Such a waste of time when she could be reading her Bible before she went to bed. But, oh no, she was

teaching them vanity instead of piety. To tell her she had
to do things different would just mean another horrid fight.
Gideon would simply wait until spring and the next wife
he had would retrain the girls to be more godly.

"Okay, girls, that's it," Gussie said. "Up to bed now. I'm
so tired I could lay down and die."

Esther's face turned the color of old ashes. Ruth bit her
lip and paled until Gussie thought the girl would faint. Abigail whimpered. Lucy threw herself on the floor, commenced to kicking and screaming, a torrent of tears bathing
her baby face.

"No, no," Lucy screamed. "You can't be tired. You can't
go off and leave us. We love you, Momma. Please don't
be tired."

"Tell us what to do, Momma," Esther grabbed her hand.
"Do you need me to help you up to the bed. Ruth can get
a wet rag and wash your face. Just tell us what to do. Don't
be tired."

"What is going on here?" Gussie asked, staring right at
the preacher.

"It's our first mother," Ruth said.

"What about Becky?" Gideon asked, bending down to
pick up Lucy, who kicked him in the nose and refused to
be touched.

"I'll take care of her," Gussie said. "Come here Lucy
and stop that screaming. If you don't, you can't use the
needle tomorrow and sew on the rags while I mend."

The tantrum stopped, yet the sobbing continued as Lucy
tried to bury her whole body into Gussie's shoulder. Esther,
Ruth, and Abigail were still glued to the living room floor,
weeping uncontrollably.

"I just said I was tired," Gussie said. "Why are you crying?"

"Our mother said that. She was standing out there in the
river with her gold pan in her hands. Lucy was over there
on the river bank in a basket," Esther said between sobs,
wiping her nose and tears with the sleeve of her dress. "Our

mother was all red in the face like you were when you come in the house while ago. And she held her back and said she was so tired she could lay down and die."

"My Lord," Gussie whispered. The poor children.

"She didn't mean it," Gideon said around the lump in his own throat.

"Yes she did," Ruth said. "She did mean it Daddy. That night she just laid down and died and we never did see her again. You took her away and we stayed with Clara and when you come back the next day, she wasn't there no more. Then you moved us into this house and she still hasn't come back. We don't want our new momma to be tired and lay down and die. We love her."

"And I love you, but that's not what happened to your mother," Gussie said.

"Yes, it is," Ruth said with a shudder.

"Well, I'm healthy as a horse and I'm not going to lay down and die, and right now I'm going to take you all four up to bed. I love all of you, too," Gussie gathered them into a big family hug.

"What did Daddy do with her?" Abigail asked.

"There was a funeral and he buried her in the ground like people do when someone dies. You know that," Gussie said gently. "You've been to her grave lots of times."

"No, I haven't," Abigail said. "You mean our mother is in the church yard in one of those kind of graves?"

Gussie looked up at the preacher, questions pouring from her eyes.

"Dust to dust. Ashes to ashes. It was over. They don't need to . . ." he began icily. "They are my children, Augusta. Not yours. Not ever yours. I'll take care of them as I see fit."

"No we are not," Esther said. "We are your daughters and we are our new momma's girls. And she'll take care of us, too, because we love her just like we love you, Daddy."

"Don't you be sassy with me," Gideon said as he turned a glaring eye toward his oldest.

"This is enough!" Gussie exclaimed. "We're all emotional tonight. Right now I'm going to take you up to bed, girls. Tomorrow after school we're going to go to the cemetery and you can see where they laid your mother to rest. She was a fine woman and what she said that day was just something she said. Being tired did not make her die. So up you go. Did I ever tell you the story of how my sister, Gypsy, stopped an Indian uprising? She saved everyone on the wagon train. Now everyone into Esther and Ruth's bed for a story and then Abigail and Lucy can go to their rooms. I'll deal with you later so don't you say a single word right now," she whispered over her shoulder to the preacher, who absolutely looked like he was sprouting horns out of all that thick hair.

Gideon seethed in his study for a half hour before he heard Gussie go to her bedroom and shut the door. So she was too chicken to come back down and face him, was she? He'd been nice to her, letting her and those overbearing women have the church for their little meetings, and this was the repayment he got? He wasn't going to bed with this heaviness in his heart. If she couldn't at least pretend to be a lady and face him in his study, then he'd take the argument to her. He took the steps two at a time and slung open her door without knocking.

She stood there in a pair of lace-edged drawers and a camisole, neither of which left much to the imagination. The softness of her skin begged his hands to touch her; the wrath in her eyes said she'd rip his heart out if he did.

"Get dressed and come down to my study in five minutes," he said.

"Forget it. I'm going to bed," she replied. "I don't have anything to say to you."

"Well, I've got plenty to say to you," he fired back. "For one thing, they were little children, Lucy only a few months old, so they didn't need to see their mother in a wooden box. They didn't need to see them shoveling dirt in on top of her. So I left them behind and I took care of it myself."

"You were wrong, Preacher. They did need to see it. They needed to be held and comforted and they needed the finality of it. They needed to be told that they hadn't caused her death. They needed that very much, because they think they made her tired and she died because of them. I know what I'm talking about. My mother died when I was born. For years and years, I overheard the relatives saying behind closed doors that I'd caused her to die. I used to lay on her grave and beg her to forgive me or come back and take me with her. Do you have any idea what it feels like to be a little girl with no mother? How bad it hurts? At least I had the grave to go to. It was all I had. They've had nothing," she said. "And I'm taking them over to the cemetery behind the church tomorrow. That is the place, isn't it? Do you ever go there and talk to her?"

"Of course, I do. She was my wife," he said forlornly.

"She's their mother and they need to have that same option," Gussie said. "Now if you'll get out of my room, I'm going to bed."

"What happened out there in the rain, it won't happen again," he said stiffly, changing the subject. "It was a moment of weakness and I shall pray that God will make me stronger. I can see why men who are unhappy at home go searching for something else."

"Like in a saloon?" Gussie asked, her voice taut with ire.

"Yes, that is the kind of woman you are, isn't it?" He turned abruptly and slammed her door.

She had her nightrail on before she remembered her plan. Well, if he could come barging into her room, then she could do the same. What was good for the goose, certainly was good for the gander too. She picked up her shawl and then threw it back on the chair. Nope, she had something to say and she'd do it just like she was. He could deal with the fact he was a weak man, who might any day go slumming in the saloons down at the other end of town.

She didn't knock but slung open the door, half expecting to find him kneeling beside the bed begging that his wanton soul not be cast into hell's everlasting fire for letting his lips touch those of a common trollop. He was sitting in a rocking chair looking out the window and turned only slightly when the door opened, expecting it to be Abigail who wanted a drink of water or who'd had a bad dream. He wore only his trousers with his suspenders hanging to the sides. His bare, muscular chest was covered in curly, downy, brown fur and Gussie wondered if it was as soft as it looked.

"Why are you here?" he asked.

She could see his jaw muscles working overtime trying to curb his tongue from another lashing out about how no decent woman would arrive in a man's room at that hour of the night wearing nothing but a white nightrail.

What he was actually thinking was that he was glad a whole room separated them because he'd never seen anyone so lovely as Augusta right at that minute. Moonlight streamed in the window, lighting up half of her beautiful face, leaving the other half in mysterious shadows. Her hair hung over her shoulders and those light, strange, blue eyes twinkled in the semi-darkness. Through the sweeping folds of the thin, gauzy night garment he could see a perfect body waiting to be loved. Yes, he was fortunate he was across the room or else his sinful human spirit might have taken over and he would have been drawn to take her in his arms.

"I almost forgot," she said so sweetly it scared him, "thank you for your generosity in giving us the church to meet in. We are grateful, and I wanted to thank you. Good night, Preacher."

She shut his door ever so gently and went back to her room. There, she'd done it. She'd spoken to him in kind tones. He could sit there in all his handsome glory and think on that the rest of the night. She was going to sleep. Tomorrow would be a long day, and guests would be arriving in the afternoon to discuss raising children. She thought, as she pulled the sheets up around her neck, perhaps next week she'd better plan on creating a meeting to discuss how to raise a husband.

Chapter Eight

A browned to perfection, roasted turkey sat in the middle of the Thanksgiving table. Connie fussed around bringing sourdough rolls, a big bowl of green beans and potatoes boiled together, corn on the cob, baked sweet potatoes, and gravy to the table. Gussie washed the little girls' hands, dried them thoroughly, and got them all seated before she called Jack and the preacher to dinner.

Jack took his place at one end of the table, motioning for Gideon to be seated at the other end. Connie sat to Jack's left with Esther and Ruth on the same bench. Gussie had been given the seat on Gideon's left with Lucy right beside her and Abigail next to her.

"We'll join hands and say grace, now," Connie said as she held her hands out to Jack and Esther. "Jack will you say it for us?"

Gideon had already bowed his head and was about to open his mouth when Connie called upon Jack to say the Thanksgiving blessing. He'd never heard of such a thing as inviting the preacher to dinner and then not asking him to say the blessing. He'd thought about his prayer all night last night, remembering all the things he would tell God he was thankful for. His neck burned with embarrassment but he quickly held out his hands, taking Ruth's in one and

87

Gussie's in the other. She must've had her hands in hot water because her palm felt unusually warm lying there in his while Jack cleared his throat and said a presentable grace even if it was a bit shorter than Gideon would have said, especially on Thanksgiving Day.

The tingles in Gussie's hand created a warmth down deep in her insides; feelings not totally unlike the kiss had stirred up. Surely she wasn't beginning to like her husband? She shook the idea from her mind. Not in a million years!

"Amen," Connie said softly. "Now Jack, you carve this magnificent bird. Isn't it wonderful that Jack had the foresight to grow up a bunch of turkeys this year? We sold nearly every one of the toms to neighbors and friends. Next year we're going to grow twice as many. You know in the warm summer, it would be nice to have turkey and it doesn't have to be potted."

"Potted?" Ruth drew her eyebrows down so much like Gideon that Gussie smiled.

"Yes, potted," Connie said, keeping up the conversation. "Did your mother ever make potted meat?"

"I don't remember. I was just four when she passed on, but Momma took us to see her grave and we put flowers on it and I talked to her. I told her all about the women comin' in the wagons and everything I could remember. Momma says that her spirit will know when I talk to her. But what is potting meat?" Ruth said. "What do you do? Like putting a petunia in a pot?"

"Somewhat," Connie answered as she passed the corn on the cob around the table while Jack carved the bird. "Sometimes you have to do something with meat to keep it from spoiling. So you get out the pickling crock and begin to fry the pork or beef or whatever you've got. First of all you pour some of the grease that cooks out of the meat into the bottom of the crock. Then you lay the meat down in the crock as it gets cooked, pouring the grease in on top of each batch. When the crock is full, you finish off with a layer of grease. It keeps the meat for about six weeks.

But you got to remember that when you stick the fork down in the jar, you got to bring up whatever is speared. Then you have to fill up the hole with more grease. That way it seals it back. So that's why it's called potted meat. With turkey, you'd just chop of his head, scald him good, pick the feathers off and roast him. A Sunday dinner crowd could eat him in one day, and there wouldn't be a problem with the meat spoiling."

"Well, I don't foresee any of this wonderful meat going to waste," Jack said, heaping everyone's plates with the tender turkey Connie had basted with two pounds of fresh cream butter.

Gideon ate with gusto, without saying a word, even though Jack, Connie, and Gussie kept up a steady conversation. Food was sustenance for the body. He'd never understand the inclination of people to have to use a meal as a social event.

"So Gideon, when do you think the war will actually begin?" Jack asked.

Gideon wiped his mouth with the napkin he'd laid properly across his knees. "Soon, I would suppose. I've got a meeting in Sacramento next week. Several preachers are going to discuss whether we will go and which persuasion we should adopt, along with other things."

"Well, while you're discussin' things," Connie said, "I'd like to know why it is we have to sit on one side of the church and our men folks on the other. We're families now, so why isn't it right for us to sit together?"

Gideon wouldn't have touched that with a ten foot pole, especially not at a holiday dinner. "I'll sure ask them about that," he said, biting into another succulent strip of turkey.

"Did you know that *Godeys Lady's Magazine* said that everyone in the United States was adopting the last Thursday in the month of November as Thanksgiving Day?" Gussie said. "The writer said that thirty states and three territories celebrated it last year, and that we should all put up a united front for the perpetual political union of the

United States by celebrating it at the same time this year. I wonder who is silly enough to think that this delicious bird can keep the North and South from a war."

"I expect it'll take more than celebrating Thanksgiving on the same day to keep this nation out of war," Connie said.

"Women shouldn't bother themselves with the worry of war," Gideon said.

"Why?" Gussie asked. "If our men all go off to defend whichever principle they believe is right, then we'll be left on the home front all alone. If we don't understand or can't bear the idea of talking about war, how will we survive? While you men are out there discussing strategy and war plans, we'll be left to take care of the children, the town, the church even. So why shouldn't we worry ourselves with the possibility of a nation at war?"

"Well said, Gussie," Connie agreed. "California will fight for the Union I would suppose?"

"Most likely, but then California is a melting pot of both the South and the North. Gold had no stipulations on which one could come and lay claim to it. If someone who owned slaves could find a mother lode then they could have it. However, if someone from the North who'd even run underground railroads for slaves found the gold first, then it didn't crawl back into the farthest corners of the mine and refuse to be dug out," Gussie said.

"Enough talk of war in front of the children," Gideon said. "Let's discuss something more pleasant today. Like how wonderful this meal is. You women folks have outdone yourselves."

Gussie's mouth flew open and for a moment she figured she'd have to pull her bottom lip up from her lap. Gideon Jefferson had just paid them a compliment on the dinner. She'd been cooking three meals a day for weeks and not a single kind word had fallen from his lips.

"Well, thank you." Connie beamed. "We are so glad you and your family could join us today. Thanksgiving should be enjoyed with friends and family. Since neither of us have family close enough to celebrate with, then it's nice to have friends."

"Sure took a lot to be able to say that about the two of us, didn't it?" Gussie asked Connie, remembering the days when she would have gladly thrown the woman under a wagon and enjoyed watching her die when it ran over her.

"Guess it did," Connie replied as she laughed. "Did Gussie tell you about our arguments?" She looked right at Gideon.

"No, I guess she didn't," Gideon said, hating the way Connie kept referring to her as Gussie.

"Well, Connie sure told me," Jack said. "She entertains me for an hour every night after we go to . . . after we retire." He blushed. "Seems she was so afraid of marriage, she thought she'd just take Rafe Pierce from Willow, who is Gussie's youngest sister. Figured if she hurried up and got married that the fear would be faced and gone. I'm sure glad she didn't succeed in her mission."

"Me too." Connie reached across the table and touched his hand possessively.

Gussie wished she had a husband that she could be that familiar with, but like one of her cousins said, "If ifs and buts were candy and nuts, we'd all have a merry day."

The little girls busied themselves with a fine meal and paid little attention to talk of war or wagon train stories. They just knew if they cleaned their plates they could have pumpkin pie for dessert, and Connie had slyly told them there would be popcorn balls in the middle of the afternoon after nap time.

A conversation started about the raising of turkeys and the profit that could be had from it and Gussie's mind wandered. Connie had taken her advice to heart and pretty curtains graced all the windows. She'd used a big floral print in the parlor and had constructed pillows of the same fabric for the rocking chairs flanking the fire place. The kitchen was brightened with red and white gingham checks that matched the table cloth trimmed with a crocheted picot edging. Above the mantle she'd arranged a few of her own things she must have had stored away in her trunk, but that vase was brand new, straight from the general store and filled to capacity with wild flowers. The one-floor house Jack had built for her had three bedrooms across the backside with room for more if the time ever came. Connie's touches had already shown up in every room and she surely seemed proud of her home as well as her husband.

Gussie thought of the parsonage and how badly it needed repairs. The preacher's study was the worst room in the place and should be the nicest. That's where he met with the deacons and elders of the church on Wednesday afternoons. It's where he spent most of his time. She really should see to redecorating the whole thing. However, that wasn't her concern. He'd already said he was sending her away as soon as the spring thaw arrived. *Not unless I want to go,* she thought, the notion as foreign to her as the idea of Gideon saying something nice about dinner. Did she want to go? No, she didn't. Not that she cared a whit about the preacher, but she'd lost her heart to the girls, her daughters. They'd said so themselves that night when Gideon forgot he was a preacher and kissed her. They'd said that they belonged to her just as much as they did to him.

Gussie had lived with lots of different relatives in the years it took to raise her. She remembered some of her aunts who had their own bedrooms. She could do that. She could stay with the preacher and adopt those four little girls as her own. She'd never have any that she could love more than them. She was as certain of that as she was that the sun would rise in the east tomorrow morning. No one would ever know that she and the preacher weren't really man and wife. They could just think she was barren and feel sorry for the man because she couldn't produce sons for him. She wondered if folks had ever had pity for him when Becky kept giving him girl children. Poor, poor preacher, who couldn't even get a son from his wonderful wife.

So could she stay even if he didn't want her? Of course, she decided. They were married and it took a big thing to bring about a divorce. She never wanted a husband anyway. What she wanted were children, and now she had them. Made her no never mind if she wasn't loved like Jack loved Connie.

The conception was barely more than the laying of a corner stone in a huge building of ideas when Lucy tugged at her sleeve. "Momma, are you all right? You're not tired are you?"

"No, my pretty baby, I'm not tired," Gussie said as she smiled sweetly at her youngest child. "Why did you ask?"

"Well, Connie asked you something two times and you didn't say nothing back to her," Abigail said. "You was smiling like you saw an angel or something."

"I did. I saw all four of you playing out there with those baby kittens," Gussie said. "I was just wool-gathering."

"Why?" Ruth said. "How was you wool-gathering while we are eating dinner?"

"It's just an expression," Gussie said.

"Whatever *were* you thinking about?" Connie laughed. "No, don't answer that. I can see just remembering whatever it was makes you blush. Mercy, I wouldn't want to answer such a question, myself."

"What did you ask?" Gussie tried to change the subject and to control the high color burning up her cheeks. Connie thought she'd been daydreaming about intimate things with the preacher. Wouldn't she be surprised to know that what she'd really been thinking was that she'd never, ever be intimate with him?

"I said, if you could have voted, would you have cast your ballot for President Lincoln?" Connie repeated.

Would wonders never cease? Gussie had figured Connie to be nothing more than a flirty little girl and now the woman was discussing all kinds of grown up things. Gussie would have to write to her four sisters and tell them the story of Thanksgiving dinner and just how much Connie had matured.

"It's a ridiculous question," Gideon said, looking down his nose at Augusta. "Women won't ever be given the vote. Women aren't capable of using their brains to determine political things, no matter what you say about having to hold down the front while the men go off to war."

"Yes, I would have voted for him," Gussie ignored him blatantly and looked across the table at Connie. "He appears to be a decent man with the best interest of our country at heart."

"But you are a southern girl. What if he frees the slaves and war comes because of it?" Connie asked.

"We weren't rich enough to have slaves. We were just hardworking poor people. Farmers, mostly. So I didn't grow up with someone to wait on me hand and foot. I don't think one person has the right to own another person, no matter what color that person's skin is. But I also don't think a nation should split over that. Surely there is some way it could be resolved without a war," she said.

"Just like a woman," Jack commented as he laughed. "Gideon, I do believe you are right. They'd want to sit down and have tea, draw up a pretty little agreement, and turn all those slaves loose to fend for themselves. They've been told what to do and how to do, had their needs met by those who owned them. How would they ever survive in the world without someone to boss them?"

"The same way we women would," Connie answered as she raised an eyebrow. "And will, when we're freed like they will be when the war comes. Perhaps someday we will have to fight a war to get our freedom. After all, we've been told what to do and how to do also. We have no rights, either. So maybe we'll all rebel someday and fight for our freedom."

"I think I just stepped in it," Jack laughed. "Forgive me darlin' and let's change this topic back around again to pumpkin pies and turkeys. Matter of fact, I think it's time for me to run down to the spring house and bring up the cream to pour over the top of those pies. How about you girls? You ready for pumpkin pie covered in cold, thick cream?"

"Yes, please!" They said in unison.

Jack and Gideon went outside to walk around the ranch following dinner. Gussie stripped the girls down to their bloomers and camisoles and told them a story before their nap, then she and Connie sat on the porch and had a visit. Their conversation did not involve war or freeing women or even giving them the right to vote.

In the middle of the afternoon they all ate popcorn balls, washed down with tall glasses of fresh lemonade from the fruit in Connie's backyard. She sent them home with a basket full of both lemons and grapefruit, and told Gussie that next summer when the grape vines were laden, they'd have plenty for juice and jelly.

Gideon could fairly well taste the jelly before he remembered that Augusta would be gone by the time the fruit ripened. She'd be gone before the first new sprigs of green found their way out of those dead vines back behind the house. He'd watched her carefully during dinner, surprised at how formal she could be. One would never guess that she'd danced in saloons. He'd always figured those women to be the ones with morals as loose as those who worked in bordellos. Something about Augusta didn't fit with that scene, though. She'd been raised by hardworking, plain people, yet she sat with her back ramrod straight, her manner flawless.

Would he want to stay married to her if she didn't have that past? He couldn't answer. Would he ask her to stay if the whole town of Washington hadn't seen her in that floozy dress? That, he wouldn't answer. To do so would mean he was judging and Gideon prided himself on his ability not to judge.

Gussie rode along in the buggy beside him, her shoulder

against his, four girls in the back chewing gum Jack had given them before they left. She could smell the fresh spruce flavor of it all the way to the front of the buggy. Was she really entertaining notions of staying in a loveless marriage to raise those rascals behind her? Yes, she was. War was coming; men would go and men would be killed. Just because the preacher wore a white collar and carried a Bible didn't mean a thing to a bullet fired into the air. It could kill him as quickly as it could kill a rifle-carrying soldier. She wouldn't leave her girls to be tossed to and fro amongst relatives. No, she'd stay. Just try to get the preacher to make her leave. She would swear to the judge that she loved him with her whole heart and that he just wanted rid of her because of her past. Lies, yes. But it might keep him from giving the preacher a decree of divorcement.

"So what are you thinking about so sternly that it makes your eyes draw into slits?" Gideon asked.

"The future," she said simply.

"Well, don't worry. Leave it to the men to worry about the war, Augusta," he said.

"War isn't a part of the future I was thinking about," she said.

"While we are talking about it, where did you read that, in *Godeys Magazine?*" he asked.

"Connie and I read it together when she visited me a few weeks ago. She got the magazine at the general store, I think. Why? I certainly didn't put it on your account there if that's what you're worried about. I've only bought food, but we do need to talk about me buying some good grade cotton to make the girls some new underwear," she said.

"You don't talk about underthings in public, Augusta. I asked about the magazine because I don't hold with women reading anything but the Bible. It is folly and breeds discontentment," he said.

"Well, *la-teee-da.*" Gussie fanned her face with the back of her hand. So much for the two of them being civil. "I'll read what I want. Connie has a copy of *The Scarlet Letter* she's going to loan me when she finishes it. She bought it at the general store too."

"You will not bring that filth into my house," he said through clenched teeth. How could he have even asked himself the foolish question concerning keeping her?

"I will read whatever I want," she whispered in a hiss. "After all, you've labeled me worse than that and I didn't even get the game to go with the name. All I did was dance a fast dance to entertain the men in a saloon. Maybe you should fashion up a big S for saloon to sew on the front of all my dresses so no one will ever forget what you can't forgive."

Chapter Nine

Twenty-seven serious men gathered in the church on the north side of Sacramento that Tuesday morning. Gideon was among them, with a question lying heavy on his soul. The first item on the agenda was whether or not they would bear arms when and if the war split the states. One minister argued that if they didn't have the means to defend themselves then they wouldn't be worth much as chaplains to the men. However, when the vote came in, there were twenty-five against taking up arms and only two for the issue. The next item of whether to incorporate Sunday school into the churches was kicked around until the clock chimed twelve times with the leader of the morning meeting tabling that issue until after the noon meal.

Gideon and his friend, Joshua, who preached in a church up in Yolo, went to one of the local hotels for lunch. Twenty foot engraved copper ceilings gleamed from the ceiling in the lobby and restaurant off to one side when the sunlight from the expanse of windows bounced off them. Gideon asked for a table for two and a waiter wearing a white shirt, starched stiffly and ironed to perfection, led them to a choice place near the front windows so they could watch the people as they ate.

"So what's on your mind, my friend?" Joshua asked.

He'd known Gideon since they'd met years ago in the gold mines. Joshua had been one of those first few who'd listened to Gideon preach out there in the wide open spaces on Sunday morning. In a brush arbor, Joshua had felt the call to go into the ministry himself. Now he was engaged to a lovely lady who reminded him in many ways of Gideon's deceased wife, Becky. She lived in Sacramento and they planned a spring wedding.

"Why did you ask that?" Gideon asked, looking over the menu the waiter had put in his hands. The seafood looked good. Maybe he'd have stuffed crabs and fried clams, along with a nice green salad and fried potatoes.

"Because I've never seen you look so miserable. Not even after Becky died," Joshua said.

"Did you hear about that wagon train of brides some of the miners paid Jake and Hank to bring back from the East?" Gideon asked.

"Sure did. Not many of us in this area or all the way to St. Jo, Missouri that ain't heard about that. Seemed like a fool idea to me to begin with. Leaving the job of finding decent women in the hands of two old wagon masters who most likely had never known a decent woman in their entire lives. And you got all those marriages right in your territory didn't you? My lands, man, no wonder you look so forlorn. Bet you've got all kinds of problems walking in your front door. Those miners must've been crazy out of their minds to try something like that. There's women in California, even if they are scarce, and it would have cost them far less to go courting outside their little area than to bring in a whole wagon train of problems," Joshua said.

The waiter appeared with two glasses of water and they gave him their orders. Gideon wiggled in his chair, wondering how to approach the subject of Augusta. He drank deeply of the cool water and wiped his mouth on the linen napkin he'd laid across his knees.

"Actually, there's only been one problem and it wasn't hard to resolve. The couple literally fell in love after one consultation and seem to be doing fine. The others are fairing well, I suppose. You see, there's this woman named Augusta who was the backbone of the whole journey. I understand she and her sisters were a bit like the leaders and kept things going well for everyone. Anyway, this Augusta, she has set up meetings for them all. If some of them can't sew, then they get together with those who can. Those who have children involved meet with others of like circumstances. I've even heard under the table that there's a meeting with one of the women who teaches the others how to flirt with their own husbands," Gideon whispered.

"Sounds like you found a jewel in this Augusta. Who did she marry?" Joshua asked.

If Gideon would have had to spit or die he'd have had to shut his eyes and hoped for the best because his mouth was suddenly as dry as if he'd just walked across the whole desert without a drop of water. "Me," he said weakly.

Joshua covered his mouth but the grin was bigger than his hand. The guffaw that followed brought several eyes toward their table and Gideon felt heat frying the back of his neck and cheeks. "That's funny, Gideon, and I didn't even know you had a sense of humor. The conference would have taken your church if they ever thought you ordered a mail order bride. Mercy, man, that's a good joke. But I'm not buying it. Not from you, who has always been straight as a sober judge and never made bad judgments. Besides, didn't I hear that the way of it was that the men drew a name from a hat and was bound to that woman. What if you drew the name of a former barmaid?" Joshua wiped his brow with his napkin.

"I did," Gideon said. "Not a barmaid but a saloon dancer."

Joshua's chest heaved with laughter, but he kept it reined in to a chuckle. "All right. Let's stop the jesting, Gideon."

"Joshua I'm telling the truth," Gideon said.

Joshua's eyes widened slightly, then they got bigger and

bigger. His friend really was telling the truth but Joshua could hardly believe it. "Why?"

"Because Becky was gone and the girls were out of hand. Lucy has a temper that would put Lucifer to shame. The miners came to me and asked if I wanted to send some gold with Hank and Jake and they promised they'd bring decent women. I could never love again, Joshua. But I needed a wife and a mother. It didn't seem like so bad a deal, then when I drew out her name, I refused to marry her."

"And?" Joshua asked, barely above a whisper.

"And Lucy threw a screaming fit. Abigail was sobbing. Esther and Ruth were upset. The men were all lined up on one side of the road and the women on the other side. When I said I wouldn't marry her, the women all started following her back to the circle of wagons just outside of town. My hands were tied. There wasn't going to be any weddings until I married the woman," Gideon explained, his voice becoming tighter and tighter with every word.

"How'd you find out she was a saloon dancer?" Joshua asked, glancing around to make sure they were the only ministers eating at that particular hotel.

"She was wearing her dancing costume. A bright red shiny dress so short her ankles showed. All trimmed up in black lace and cut low in the front. Her hair, which is a combination of blonde and brown, was hanging down her back and she had this shiny thing in her hair with black feathers hanging from it," Gideon said.

"Then everyone there knows?" Joshua's face skewed up in disbelief.

"Every one of them. And the funny thing is they think she's some kind of angel or something. Every one of them women treat her like she's the queen. My daughters love her. Called her Momma from day one. She keeps a house like no other woman I've ever seen, and she can cook like a chef," Gideon said.

"Does she dress like that every day?" Joshua asked.

"Oh, no. Haven't seen that red dress since she took it off that day. She sleeps in the guest room. I can't bring myself to make her my real wife in the biblical sense. It would be such a dishonor to Becky's memory," Gideon said.

"Then what are you worried about?" Joshua asked. "Everyone has probably forgotten about the dress and the conference members don't know about it, so you can just wait until next year and tell them that you've married. No one ever needs to know what really happened, do they?"

"No, but I don't want to stay married to her. I want a divorce so I can find a decent woman. One to be a real wife to me," Gideon said. "I'm going to bring up the issue of divorce and see what the council says this afternoon."

"Are you going to tell them about Augusta?" Joshua asked.

"Of course not. I'm just going to remind them of the fact that a hundred men and women just got married and there is sure to be some dissension amongst them," Gideon said.

"Don't expect miracles, Gideon," Joshua said.

"That's what it will take for me to be rid of her, isn't it?" Gideon asked.

"I think one of the highest calling," Joshua nodded.

The miracle didn't materialize.

Gideon began the meeting that afternoon. He briefly told the other twenty-six members of the conference about the situation in the town of Washington. With so many newly married couples, there was bound to be some who became disenchanted with their situation and came to him for advice about divorce. Joshua kept his head down, barely looking up at Gideon. He couldn't in all good conscience raise his hand and vote to give Gideon permission to advise people to divorce. It just wasn't done. Society frowned upon it and the church refused to acknowledge even the notion. Only in extreme cases of proven adultery would the council even consider it.

"You know where we stand on that issue," Floyd, the oldest preacher in the council said. "If they went into this bizarre situation with the idea that they would end it if it didn't work, then they were foolish men and women. We can put it to the vote but it's senseless. That's a moral issue which we can not allow. To let these rash men and women end their marriages and still be accepted into the church and by it would be asking for trouble. You can do nothing if they insist upon decrees of divorcement. That's for the judge of the land to decide. However, divorced people cannot be part of the church."

"While the question is still open, let us discuss the possibility of what would happen in our council if a preacher were to ask for a divorce?" Gideon said.

"Do we have one who is in that situation?" Floyd asked.

"I don't know, but I thought I'd ask," Gideon said.

"Well, I suppose we can address it. A preacher has to maintain the highest of high standards for his congregation. If a man erred in judgment in that area and felt he couldn't keep his wife, then I would stand on the platform that he could never preach in the church again. The example would be tainted. He could scarcely tell his congregation that they weren't welcome in the church if he, himself, were a divorced man, now could he?" Floyd said.

"Then do we need to vote on the issue at all?" Joshua asked.

"No, I guess we don't," Gideon said. "Shall we go back to the idea of Sunday school? When we have the money to build rooms onto our church buildings for such a thing, do we allow women to teach in the classes?"

"No," Floyd said. "A woman can bring up her children in a godly home and teach them there, but not in the church. If we let them wedge a foot in the door in that instance then before long they'd want more. Before you knew it, they'd want to preach from the pulpit. The way to keep down these women's rights issues is to nip the whole thing in the bud."

Thank goodness Augusta isn't sitting in this room, Gideon thought. *She would bring fire and brimstone upon these men's heads.*

"All right, then, when the time comes that we can incorporate Sunday school into services, then it is agreed that men shall teach the classes?" Gideon asked.

Everyone nodded approval.

"How about the tiny babies? We will have young mothers and fathers who come to the Sunday school classes with little babies. Should the mothers keep them by their sides until they are of a certain age, say four years old, and old enough to understand the simple Bible stories?" Gideon asked.

"Yes," Joshua said. "That's a good idea. They need to be trained before they're old enough for classes. Men folks wouldn't want to change diapers."

That brought a few chuckles.

"I have one more question to bring before the council," Gideon said. "It concerns the possibility of men and wives sitting together in church. Some of my congregation come from backwoods churches that have permitted families to sit together."

"No," Floyd said. "Out of the question. It would breed familiarity in a holy place. Men and women sitting side by side? Why, the men would soon be putting their arms around their wives or holding their hands. Not the kind of thing for the younger people to see in a house of God. Shall we vote on it?"

The one pro vote belonged to Gideon. Twenty-six voted against it.

"My questions are answered. Joshua would you like to take the stand, now? I understand you have some members of your church who are questioning whether or not there should be an organ or piano in the church building," Gideon said as he dragged his heavy heart back to his seat. He couldn't stay married to her and keep any kind of peace in his heart. He couldn't divorce her and keep his church. Talk about being smashed between a rock and a hard place. And for the life of him he couldn't understand why a woman could be a school teacher and not a Sunday school teacher or what it would hurt for families to sit together in church.

Gussie crawled up on the ladder with a long length of wallpaper doubled back on itself. She stretched out to her full height and slapped it on the wall close to the ceiling, working with it gently all the way to the floor. Lucy had her hands on her hips like she'd seen Gussie do so many times and watched mesmerized, her little head thrown back as far as she could get it so she could see all the way to the top of the twelve foot wall. She clapped her hands and hopped on one foot when the strip of pale blue paper with cream colored shocks of wheat was in place.

"There's the first one," Gussie said, climbing down from the ladder. She wore an old pair of drawers with patches on the knees and rear end, a rag around her head and a shirt waist that had seen better days. To work in skirt tails would be asking for trouble. If she fell from the ladder because her feet got tangled up in her skirt tails it would terrify the girls. Besides there was no one in the house but Abigail, Lucy, and Gussie. No one would ever know she'd worked all day dressed like that.

"Pretty, Momma," Lucy said.

"Well, thank you. I hope your father likes it," Gussie said, feeling a cold dread over facing Gideon when he came home and found his study completely redone. He'd most likely pitch a fit, telling her that she hadn't asked him before she redecorated. But the job would be done and if he didn't like it, he could peel all the paper away and have his dark old dungeon back just like it was.

"Daddy will love it," Abigail said.

"Well that's just the first strip. Now we'll do it again and again until the whole room is papered and then we'll put up that pretty striped border. It's time for you girls to brush on the paste again," she said, handing them a couple of brushes she'd bought at the general store along with the wall paper.

By the time the older girls came running in the door after school, she had the paper on the walls, the border up and was halfway up the stairs going toward her room to wash up and change clothes. Esther and Ruth threw open the front door, giggling and bringing Cecil right behind them.

"Come right in Cecil. Momma's going to be so happy to see that machine thing. She's told us last night it was coming but we didn't think it'd be here until tomorrow morning after we went to school," Esther said, motioning for Cecil to come on into the living room.

"Momma, Momma, the store man is bringing your machine thing in the house," they shouted in unison.

Gussie hurried up the stairs as fast as she could, hoping all the time that Cecil hadn't seen her in her unmentionables. She stuck her head out the bedroom door and yelled down the stairs to tell Cecil to put the sewing machine in the living room and she'd take care of it later.

"I'll just wait, Mrs. Jefferson," he yelled from the bottom of the stairs. "It's almighty heavy and I'll need to set it where you intend to keep it."

"Well, shoot," Gussie exclaimed, jerking her blouse off and slipping a dress over her dirty underthings. She patted at her hair, hoping it didn't look too bad, and went down to the living room. She hadn't even thought about where she wanted the sewing machine. It couldn't be put in the study because the noise would drive the preacher insane, and she didn't want to be limited as to when she could sew anyway. There wasn't room in the kitchen, nor in her bedroom. Besides she'd probably be drawn and quartered if she let old Cecil bring a sewing machine in her bedroom when the preacher was out of town.

"Where do you want this thing?" Cecil asked, looking up at her from the newel post.

"How about in the corner, over there under the window," she said. "That way it won't be too close to the fireplace and it'll give me a fine east sunlight to sew by in the mornings."

"Sounds like a good place to me," he said, tugging the heavy treadle sewing machine to the place she'd pointed to. "How about that, girls? Your new momma going to make you up a bunch of pretty Sunday frocks?"

"No," Abigail said from the door of the study where she'd been studying the pretty blue wall paper. "She's going to make my daddy some pretty curtains for his study."

"Well, that's nice," Cecil said. "Thank you for the order, ma'am. I'm right glad it's come in so soon."

"Thank you, sir, for delivering it right to the door and bringing it in for me," she said. "Jack would have been glad to pick it up for me tomorrow when he and Connie come into town. But now that it's here I can begin to sew up those curtains tonight."

"Good day to you then," Cecil said.

"And to you," Gussie said, shutting the door behind him.

"Momma, your hands are shaking," Esther said.

"Did he see me?" Gussie asked.

"Of course he did, Momma. You stood right there and talked to him," Ruth said. "Can we have some cookies?"

"No, I mean did he see me on the steps before I got to my bedroom?" Gussie whispered.

"In her underwear," Abigail said. "She wore her bloomers and a blouse so she could make Daddy's room all pretty for him."

"No, we didn't even see you and we was ahead of him," Esther said.

"Thank the Lord," Gussie sighed. "Now let's get me and these two little ones cleaned up, then we'll all have cookies and milk. I've got a pot of soup for supper and afterwards you can all help me make curtains."

"Would Daddy be mad if Mr. Cecil saw you?" Esther asked.

"I don't know, but I would sure be upset. It's not decent for a man to see a woman in her underthings," Gussie said.

"Daddy sees us in ours when he helps us get dressed," Ruth said seriously.

"That's different. Daddy's can see their daughters when they're just little girls in their nightrails and such. It would be embarrassing for a man to see a woman like that. I never dreamed of him delivering that machine with no one else here but me and you girls," Gussie said.

"Well, he didn't see nothing," Esther said. "Now come on Abigail and I'll wash your hands. Then we can have cookies."

Gussie sighed again. The preacher would literally kill her if he knew she was running around in her underwear with the front door unlocked. She sure didn't want him mad at her right then, not when she'd made up her mind that she was staying in California.

Chapter Ten

On Thursday morning Gideon drove his buggy back into Washington. He still didn't have all the problems of Gussie sorted out but then he didn't have to get them in their right places today. Today he was just anxious to get home and see his daughters. At last year's conference he'd had to take them with him and depend on one of the wives of the other preachers to watch them in the day while he attended meetings. Never had he been away from them for four whole days. He missed Lucy's mischievous giggle. He wanted to feel Abigail's arms around his neck in a bear hug. The twins would be home from school in an hour and they'd come through the door in a rush of wind looking for him. And if he was totally honest with himself, he'd missed Augusta. Not that he was in a frame of mind for that much honesty right then, but perhaps they could work out some kind of agreement. She could be a housekeeper and baby-sitter and he'd pay her for her duties.

"Well, would you look at this, Cecil," Ralph said when he looked up and saw Gideon in the doorway. "The prodigal preacher has returned home."

"I sure have," Gideon said. "Buggy is out there, Ralph. Horse is hungry. I don't think those big city liveries take care of animals the way you do."

"Thank you," Ralph grinned. "Guess you'll be anxious to get on home to them pretty girls of yours and that saloon wife."

"What did you say?" Gideon cut his dark eyes around to the man.

"When the cat's away the mice will play," Cecil used the old adage with a sneer on his face. "Or do you know about the shenanigans that go on and just let it go by?"

"Would you be a little more specific in what you are saying?" Gideon asked, that prickly itch on his neck forewarning that something wasn't right at all in his home.

"Sure will. Your wife done ordered up one of them fancy new sewing machines. She thought it was going to come in on Tuesday morning but it got here on the freight wagon on Monday so I just thought I'd do her a good deed and take it on over there. She'd said Jack and Connie would bring it, but I figured she might want to do a bit of sewing so I just took it to her," Cecil drew out the story.

"And?" Gideon asked.

"Well, your two bigger girls come in from school about then and they just held the door open for me and told me to go right in. Know what I saw right there with my own two eyes, Gideon?" Cecil asked.

"Of course I don't know," Gideon said crossly. "How could I? I was in Sacramento."

"I saw your saloon wife on the stairs in nothing but her drawers. She was barefoot and her hair was all a mess. She was wearing a shirtwaist. It was like she'd just shed her petticoats and skirt for some reason. Now why does a woman shed those? You tell me what's been going on right there in your house while you been gone. I asked her where she wanted me to put the sewing machine, figuring she'd want it in the spare bedroom where most women sew. But oh, no, she sure didn't want me up those stairs. She told me to put it right there in the window. She was all flushed and like I said her hair was a mess. Is that any way for a woman to be behaving herself with two little girls in the house?"

"I see." Gideon clenched his hands into fists of pure, unadulterated anger. Well, he'd prayed for a valid reason to divorce the woman. Adultery was the only one the church recognized and now he had it. Witnesses and all. He just wondered who the man was. "I suppose I'll go on home now and set my house to rights. Tomorrow I've planned a trip to the mines, Ralph. If you'd have my buggy ready about nine o'clock?"

"I'll do it. Right sorry to be the bearers of bad news, Gideon. That's what happens though when a preacher marries up with a saloon girl," Ralph said.

"I guess it is," Gideon said, noticing an empty place where his heart had been only moments before. How would he ever explain this to his daughters? They loved her so much, they'd be heartbroken. And Lucy? Oh, Lord, what would he do with Lucy? His step was hurried as he left the livery and crossed the street, the parsonage in view with Jack's buggy sitting out front. Was it Jack? Had all that indecent advice she'd given him about keeping his shirt off caused him to sneak around behind the preacher's back and make a cuckold of him?

By the time Gideon reached the front door his face was scarlet with anger. He half expected to sling open the door and find his wife in Jack's arms. But what he found was Augusta standing at the foot of the stairs, a smile on her face as if she was actually happy to see him.

"I've just come from the livery," he said, drawing his eyebrows down over his dark eyes in anger. "Where's Jack?"

"Jack's not here. Why would Jack be here? Abigail and Lucy saw your buggy go past a few minutes ago and . . . oh, you saw the buggy. Connie is here. She's had to make a run down back to the outhouse. She should be back any minute," Augusta said.

Before Gideon could say another word, Connie opened

the back door and yelled inside. "I just saw his buggy parked at the livery so he's home, Gussie. I can't wait to see his face when you tell him."

"Tell me what, that you've been spending my money on a sewing machine when you didn't even ask permission to buy it?" Gideon snarled.

"I didn't need to ask permission since I spent my own money on that sewing machine. I don't charge things to your account without asking you if it's all right." The smile left her face. Why did he have to come in like a raging bull over a sewing machine?

"Then tell me. Tell me about how you've played me for a fool when I was good enough to marry you even though you're nothing but a low-down saloon girl. Like I said before, leopards never change their spots, do they? You'll always be a cheap barmaid, Augusta. Now tell me who is it that you've had in my house in front of my girls. Tell me his name?" Gideon said between clenched teeth.

"What are you talking about?" Gussie asked.

"Don't you play dumb with me woman. I'm not a fool. Cecil saw you in nothing but your unmentionables when he delivered that machine, and you wouldn't let him take it up to the spare bedroom where most women sew. So who was in there that you didn't want him to see? And you doing it all right in the same house with my daughters. Get out of my house," he exclaimed while pointing dramatically to the front door.

"I think I should have the right to explain," Gussie said.

"You don't know what happened," Connie stepped in the middle of the fight. "You pig-headed fool. Listenin' to that Cecil tell tall tales. I bet he was down at Ralph's this time of day and left the store with his wife. Well, listen to Gussie's side of what happened and open your eyes, Gideon."

"I'm not listening to nothing. Not one thing. Get out of my house Augusta. Don't even pack your things. I'll have Cecil deliver them to wherever it is you are going. I don't ever want to see your face again. I plan on having divorce papers drawn up with the word adultery written all over them. That's what happens when you read trashy magazines and novels. That's what happens when I have the silly notion I can make a silk purse from a sow's ear. Now, go!"

"Yes, she'll go. Right home with me, Preacher Jefferson," Connie took Gussie's arm and led her toward the door.

Gussie followed, a cold, icy numbness settling in the core of her soul. She turned around at the door and glared at him. "Your daughters are waiting in your study. They have a surprise for you. The older two will be home in an hour. Tell them all I love them."

"I'll not tell them anything about you ever again. You are even more dead from this day forth than their natural mother," Gideon said.

"When you realize that you are a fool, she'll be at my house. If you have an apology hiding in that egotistical heart of yours, you can come around. If you aren't bringing an apology, then don't come. You're not welcome," Connie said.

"There's not a man in this town who wouldn't do just what I've done," Gideon said. "Not a one. They'll all stand beside me on this issue. None of us like to be made fools of."

"We'll see about that. You may be preaching to an empty church come Sunday," Connie said, slamming the door in his face.

"Come on Gussie. I'll send Jack for your things later this evening," Connie said. "We should've made our stand on the wedding day and insisted he draw another name since he was so dead set against marrying you. Heaven help me, though, if he'd drawn my name, I would have just died on the spot."

Gussie didn't say a word. How could she live without her four daughters? Why would he believe such an outlandish story when she'd done nothing but work from daylight to dark since she'd gotten there? Because of her past, he didn't trust her, and without trust there could never be any kind of marriage. Not even a platonic one in which she slept in her room, and he in his. But she'd never done anything to make him not believe her word and she'd given her vow that day to love and honor him. Honor meant keeping herself true and she'd done that.

Gideon stomped his foot in a childish gesture and tried to get control of himself before he went into the study where his two younger daughters waited. He'd have to tell them something but he wouldn't think of that right now. For now, they could simply believe that Augusta had gone home with Connie for the afternoon. He'd worry about the rest of it later that evening.

Finally, he took a deep breath and opened the door to find Abigail and Lucy sitting quietly in chairs right in front of his desk. For a moment he just stared at them in all their innocent beauty, then he began to see the difference in the room. It was so much lighter. How did that happen?

"Daddy, Daddy," Abigail was off the chair and wrapped around his legs. "Just look at the surprise we made you. Ain't it pretty?"

"Daddy!" Lucy threw herself into his arms. "Flour and water tastes awful but it makes the paper stay."

"What are you talking about?" He asked, the rage finally scaling off his eyes and the changes in the room becoming evident.

"Just look, Daddy," Abigail said.

And he did. New wallpaper with a masculine touch in the wheat shocks instead of flowers. Curtains of the same color as the wheat. Blue and white striped cushions in the chairs which all matched now with a fresh coat of buttercream colored paint. On his desk, on the backside of a piece of scrap wallpaper, was a note from all the girls. Esther and Ruth had drawn a house with stick people out to one side, a woman and a man and four little girls. Beside it they'd written, "Welcome home, Daddy." Abigail had added her message with a picture of the sun painted no doubt with the paint from the chairs. The letters were scribbly but it was evident her own hand had written them, probably with Augusta showing her how. "I love you, Daddy," it said. Lucy had simply used the flour and water paste to glue old buttons in strange places. Her scribbled message couldn't be read but under it in a fine hand were the words, "I missed you, Daddy," where Augusta had translated the wiggly lines.

"And we helped with it," Lucy said.

"And Momma took off her petticoats and skirts 'cause she was 'fraid she'd fall off the ladder," Abigail said seriously. "You're not mad at her for taking them off are you, Daddy."

"We'll talk about that later," he said, the emptiness in his heart growing to gigantic proportions.

"Well, the store man brung the sew thing out there and she was going upstairs and she was 'fraid he might see her. Esther and Ruth, they let him in without knockin' so she didn't know he was there. She asked Esther and Ruth if he saw her 'cause she was runnin' upstairs real fast, but they said he didn't 'cause they didn't. But she said it wasn't decent for a man to see a woman like that. What's decent, Daddy?" Abigail asked.

Connie showed Gussie to one of the spare bedrooms and told her to rest for a while. Connie brought her crochet basket from the living room and sat in a rocker beside the bed. Gussie hadn't said a word since they'd left the parsonage. For that preacher to accuse her so falsely without giving her an opportunity to tell what really happened was inexcusable. Gussie could just live with her and Jack until she figured out where she wanted to go. They'd be glad to take her in and give her a home.

Gussie's eyes blinked periodically and her chest rose and fell as she breathed. Two natural gestures, but Connie feared that she'd just seen a Dulan woman broken. And Gussie, at that. Never in her wildest imagination would she have ever believed that Gussie Dulan could be torn down. Not even by a preacher with a wicked, evil tongue, and a spirit to match. Could Gussie be with child? Was that the reason she was so despondent that she wouldn't even speak?

"Gussie," Connie said softly, curiosity worrying her senseless in the last hour, "are you with child?"

Gussie began to giggle. Tears rolled down her cheeks in streams at first then the dam broke and they bathed her face in a torrent. "I can't be pregnant, Connie," she said. "I've never even slept with him. We have separate bedrooms. He thinks I'm not worthy to be his wife. He was going to send me away when the spring thaw came anyway."

"Oh, no, but you love him," Connie said. "I could see it in your face when you were waiting on him to come home from the trip. You've been antsy all day just waiting for him. You've had your fights, but then haven't we all. Besides you had it double hard since he was such a horse's rear end at the marriage and has fought with you on everything since then. But how could you stay there? Oh, Gussie, I am so sorry. I should've seen it and rescued you a long time ago. You're welcome here forever and you know it," Connie said as she left the rocking chair and hugged Gussie tightly, letting the tears fall on the shoulder of her dress as her best friend's heart shattered over and over again.

"I don't love him," Gussie sobbed.

"Yes, you do, and that's the crying shame of it all. But we're survivors, Gussie. You and I are survivors. We made it the whole way out here and we'll survive this, too."

"Yahoo," a voice came from the front door.

"It's just Berdie." Connie brushed away a sympathetic tear from her own cheek.

"Connie, Gussie, where are you?" Berdie came right in without an invitation. "I've come to lend my support."

"She knows," Gussie whispered, trying desperately to stop crying and put on a better face. "How did she find out?"

"Everyone knows," Berdie said. "Ralph and Cecil's been spreading it like wildfire all day. We figured the preacher would come home and kill them both for their wild talk. Instead he believed them. They're down at the store right now telling everyone who comes in the store. The brides are all outside waiting to see what we need to do about this."

"All of them?" Gussie asked.

"Hey, we're more than friends. We've fought Indians, buried friends, did without water, crossed raging rivers and we lived to make it here. We might not be sisters of the flesh, but we're sure sisters of the heart and there ain't no one going to accuse one of us falsely like that and get away with it scot-free," Berdie said.

"Gideon will," Gussie said flatly.

"Just because he's a preacher? I don't think so. A preacher has to have a congregation or he don't have a church." Berdie wagged her finger at Gussie.

"The men will give him a congregation," Connie said. "They'll stick together just as much as we will. He said there wasn't a one of them that wouldn't stand beside him."

"Well, I've got different ideas. They've gotten dependent on us, you know. They like their houses all neat and clean. They like their shirts ironed and their beds changed more than once a year. And they sure enough like three meals a day set before them. Come on you two, we've got some plans to make and the Ladies Auxiliary is part of it."

They followed her out to the porch where there did indeed wait almost a hundred other women. Stern faces, some with tears, others with determination, stared back at Gussie. She could have kissed everyone of them on the cheek just for being there.

"We've made up our minds while you were in there," Viola said. "The wagons are still sitting in the yard down at the livery stable. I'm going down there and renting every one of them. I'm going to tell Ralph to circle them up just like they were the day he bought them. He should have the job done by nightfall. Then we're all going back to the circle until the preacher apologizes to Gussie. We're standing behind you girl, not just for you, but for all of us. It could've been any of us that this happened to and those men need to realize that we've got a few rights. One being that we have the right to explain. The other that we have the right to walk out. Although they may think so, we're not slaves. We're wives and we'll be treated with respect or we won't be there," Viola said.

Heavy applause followed her speech.

"I can't let you do that," Gussie said. "It's not fair to the men folks who wouldn't act like that."

"One rotten potato can sure spoil the whole basket," April said.

"And it makes the whole house stink," Connie said. "If we let this go by then our whole town will stink. We'll live in fear of what any little thing might be misconstrued as. Gussie and I will be at the circle at six o'clock. I'll load the buggy with food and tell Jack he can pick it up at the livery."

"Me, too. I baked today, as did we all, I'm sure. Bring your mending. We might be there for a while, and bring a change of clothes. We'll be circled up by the river so we can keep the washing done like we did on the journey," April said. "Let's go home now ladies. Tonight we can visit around the communal soup pot, again."

"Viola, tell Ralph to put the rent for those wagons on the preacher's bill," Gussie called out as they all were leaving.

A hushed giggle went up from the crowd.

"I can't really let them do this," Gussie said when she and Connie were back in the house.

Connie set about packing a valise with two changes of clothing. Thank goodness there wasn't much difference in her and Gussie's size. She set it aside when it was filled with the barest of necessities, then prepared two bedrolls:

a sheet, two blankets each because the nights could be really chilly, and two pillows, rolled into a long log-like tube and tied with scraps of cloth. After that she went to the kitchen, filled a wooden crate with all the bread she'd baked that day, several pounds of dry beans and a slab of bacon she'd been going to slice for supper. "If we run out of food, I'll simply go to the store and charge it on Jack's bill," she mumbled.

"I'm telling you I cannot let you or them do this," Gussie insisted.

"You have no say so, Gussie Dulan Jefferson," Connie said, a bit of that old sassy flame rekindled. "This isn't just for you even though we love and respect you. It's for us all. Call it the first convention of the Washington Women's Circle of Rights if you want to. If we don't fix it, it'll stay broke and none of us want to face a husband who's listened to nasty lies and believed them. None of us want to have our husbands throw us out and not even let us say a word. We'll have some rights in this town, or we'll live in wagons until spring thaw."

"Thank you," Gussie said humbly. "Will Jack be home by the time we leave?"

"No, but I'll leave him a note which I'm fixin' to write at this minute. So you can load all this while I do it. I hadn't even unhitched the horse yet so that's a job we won't have to do. And when you get that done, go down to the smoke house and get that ham. We'll take it, too," Connie said.

"I mean it, thank you," Gussie said.

"I know you mean it." Connie stopped long enough to hug her. "I know it down deep in my heart. You'd do the same for me. At least you would now. A few months ago you'd have thrown me in a river of alligators. And I would have loved to watch you fall off a cliff and die. But some- how it's all changed now. So let's value what we've got and get this show on the road. Gussie Dulan never was one to delay a show, now was she?"

"Never." Gussie smiled.

Connie giggled; their Gussie hadn't been whipped. Not yet, and as long as she survived, the rest of them could.

Chapter Eleven

The sheriff of Washington stood in the midst of a hundred women that evening and insisted they go home to their husbands. Several of the men had come to him asking what their rights were in an instance of pure insanity and he'd told them they had the right to discipline their wives according to the written law.

"You told them that?" Viola asked. "That they could discipline us like we were nothing but wayward children?"

The sheriff stretched himself to his full five and a half feet, puffed out his barrel chest, and nodded. "Yes I did. The law states that a man has the right to discipline his wife with a reasonable instrument."

"You mean as in whip us?" Berdie had a hard time keeping the laughter shaking her chest from erupting into a full guffaw.

"Yes, that's what the law says. It says a reasonable instrument. I looked that up in the books and a bull whip is considered a reasonable instrument. Now the husbands which you all vowed to love, honor and obey have sent me with this order. Come home now and there won't be any chastisement," he said.

"You can go back and tell those men that if they come down here with intentions like that, there'll be a mass funeral tomorrow and we'll all be widows. There ain't no man going to lay a hand on me like I was a little girl." Marlee, the largest woman in the group stepped forward and shook her finger at him. "I don't care what the law says. You got room to put every one of us in your jail for breaking the law, Mr. Sheriff? You got a wife at home that you beat with a bull whip?"

"I've got a wife at home, yes, and three small sons. I don't have to beat her. She knows her place," he said stoically.

"She sure does," a thin voice said behind him. "And it's right here with these women. Cecil is a mule's rear end for what he's done and I'm joining these women. The boys haven't had supper yet, by the way. I suggest you get on home and cook some or they'll get testy."

"You go home, woman," he pointed his finger at his wife. "You aren't going to join this bunch of hooligan women."

"Oh, yes, I am. Gussie is right. They're right. And you are all wrong. When Gideon comes down here and makes his apologies, I'll go home. By the way, James was already whining about being hungry. You know how mean-natured he is when he's hungry," she said.

"I'll go get that bull whip," he threatened.

"And I'll take it away from you and beat you to a bloody pulp with it," she cried as she snapped her hands on her hips and faced him down. A big woman, twice the size of Marlee, she was, with a bun at the nape of her neck and eyes flashing.

"Ladies," she turned around and faced them all. "I've come to ask permission to join you. I do believe it's high time us women at least had the right to open our mouths and explain. All of us know what Gussie was doing in her unmentionables. We've done it ourselves when we've had to crawl up on a ladder and hang paper. So which way are my wagonmates?"

The sheriff threw his hands up in despair and waddled

on back toward town. Supper, and dishes. Getting three rowdy boys to bed without their mother's heavy hand to take care of matters. Breakfast tomorrow morning and fixing their lunches before they went to school. Lord, he wished he could just run away.

Two fires had sprung up in the middle of the circle. A huge cauldron of beans hung above one fire and one of vegetable soup above the other. There was bread aplenty to go with their supper and Clara, the sheriff's wife, had brought along a crate with a huge round of homemade cheese in it. The aroma of the boiling beef and vegetables wafted across the town, making many men's mouths water as they awkwardly tried to prepare a lonely supper for themselves or one for a bunch of kids who had already began to whine about their new mother's being gone.

Lucy was one of the whiners.

"But Daddy where is Momma? She said she'd come in the room when you'd seen it and we'd hugged you and she wasn't there anymore and where is she?" Abigail asked over a supper of hard fried eggs and burnt biscuits.

"You was mean to her," Lucy said. "You yelled and run her off. I heard you."

"Augusta is with the other women at the river where the wagons were circled up. She and the other women are having a couple of days of Auxiliary meetings down there. You know how I went away to the church meetings, well, she's away at her meetings," Gideon said, hoping the Lord didn't strike him dead on the spot for lying.

"I'm going," Lucy said, pushing her plate back and getting up from the table.

"No, you are not," Gideon raised his voice and she puckered up.

"Yes, I am," her chin quivered and her body shook, a tantrum already in the making. "Momma needs me. She might get tired and die."

At that the other three began to weep.

"Are you going to fix our hair for school?" Esther asked between sobs.

"I don't know how," Gideon said. "But there are ironed dresses in your wardrobes. She left you clothes for tomorrow all done up."

"I'm not going to school with straight hair," Ruth said. "I'm going to stay in bed all day. I feel a headache coming on."

"Me, too," Esther exclaimed as she dramatically placed the back of her hand on her forehead. "And fever, too. I'm going to bed right now. You can wash the dishes, Daddy. I'm too sick."

"Don't you tell me what you will do. I'm the father in this house," he shouted, ashamed at himself instantly for taking his frustrations out on the girls.

"I want my momma!" Lucy stomped the floor twice then fell over and began a caterwauling that would put a hungry coyote to shame. "You get my momma. She died, didn't she?"

That set off even more sobs from the other three who promptly ran up the stairs and slammed the bedroom door. Gideon picked his youngest up from the floor and held her against his shoulder, shushing her with a soft voice.

It didn't work. She kicked, squirmed, and wiggled until he finally released her and she ran up the stairs on chubby little legs to join her sisters. He sat down in his chair and put his head in his hands. He'd really stepped in it, as Jack has so aptly put it at the Thanksgiving dinner. Not once had he considered the idea that Augusta might be innocent of the blatant lies Cecil had fabricated. Because she'd danced in saloons, he'd just figured her for a loose woman. Other than wearing a red satin dress that was six inches too short, she'd never displayed one other trait that would lead him to believe she wasn't honest and forthright. So why had he believed Cecil?

Because you wanted a divorce and that would give it to you. Because you are a complete fool who probably isn't going to apologize for his transgressions. The prayer says to forgive the trespassers. Well, you done stepped in it so deep, she won't ever forgive you so don't even try to apologize, his conscience told him flatly.

He finally went upstairs to find all four girls asleep in one bed, still wearing their clothing and shoes. He left them that way because to wake them would just bring on more tears and more questions to which he had no answers. He washed up in cold water from the basin in his room and stretched out on the bed. The moon was a big, round, white ball in the sky. What was Augusta thinking as she looked at the same moon from under a wagon? No doubt, she wasn't thinking that she owed him even a moment of time for him to explain why he'd been so angry. He'd blown any chance of her staying in his house as a sitter and house-keeper right out of the sky with his accusations. He rolled over to face the far wall so he wouldn't have to share the moon with Augusta.

"Be honest," he whispered to himself. *I can't,* he thought. *It would hurt too bad to admit that if I didn't love her I wouldn't have gotten so angry. If there were no feelings for her then I would have simply laughed it off and told those men that she was just a common trollop and I planned to pack her out of Washington on the first stage leaving town after the spring thaw. I can't admit that to my heart because it's already breaking, and I have no chance now to rectify a thing. Saying I'm sorry is just plain old words. God sent me a wife, a wonderful woman. Even if she had a past, of all the people in this whole state a preacher should have forgiven it. Well, God, I thank you, but it's too late.*

He slept fitfully until just after dawn, awakening with half an expectation of hearing Lucy come running into his room and bouncing on his bed, telling him that breakfast was ready. When his eyes were fully opened, he realized it had just been the fragments of the end of a dream. Not only was breakfast not ready, the supper dishes with dried eggs on them were still sitting on the table. He moaned and threw his feet over the side of the bed.

He stuffed burnt biscuits from the night before with jam for their breakfast and threw a couple in a bucket for the twins and sent them off to school, thankful at least that they'd be out of his hair for the day. He washed Lucy's face and endured her mean looks. What would Augusta do on Friday? Maybe he could set the girls busy at a job and they'd forget about Augusta. Fat chance. He shook his head. Today was Friday. She'd be catching up on the odd jobs and baking. He wasn't about to stir up cookies or pies. No, the children could play in their rooms with their dolls.

"I'm going to Momma," Lucy said.

"No, little lady, you are not." Gideon squatted down on his heels so he would be on her level. "Augusta is at that meeting and there's no kids allowed."

"You did it. She took me," Lucy said.

"Not this time," Gideon told her. "Now you and Abigail go up to your room and play with your dolls."

"Esther and Ruth didn't make their beds up like Momma said. And they throwed their underthings under the bed, and they said if you didn't like it you could go get Momma. They said you made her go away because she fixed your study." Abigail tilted her head to one side and looked down her nose at him while she tattled.

"Children don't know everything," he said softly. "It's a complicated issue, Abigail. It's hard to explain to a four-year-old."

"Why?" she asked.

Before he could answer Esther and Ruth ran through the door and into the living room. Why on earth did six-year-old children think they had to run everywhere? He wondered. "What are you doing home?" He asked.

"Miss Harris said for us to all go home. She's not teaching no more school to any of us until you men take care of your business. That's what she said to tell our daddies when we got back home. She said she's going to the circle of wagons and joining the women there and there wouldn't be no school. So we get to come home and play all day," Esther said.

"What did she mean, Daddy? You men and your business?" Ruth asked.

"Nothing that you would understand," he said. "Go on up to your room. I understand you didn't make your beds or pick up your dirty things this morning? I expect you to act like you did when Augusta was here."

"Then bring her back," Esther said, running up the stairs.

The women had just finished eating a breakfast of sliced ham and scrambled eggs when they saw a buggy coming down from town. It stopped outside the circle and a lone woman got out, picked up a bag, and approached the camp. Silence met her. She stopped just outside the wagons and called out to Viola.

"Hello, Miss Harris," Viola yelled. "Come on in. We don't bite."

"Thank you," she said, hiking her skirt tails over the wagon tongue and joining the others. "I am Myrtle Harris. Those of you who have children will know me because I'm the teacher at the Washington school and have been for five years. Ralph Harris is my father. My mother died a couple of years ago. If you don't want me here, Augusta, I'll leave. I could understand, with the way my father has acted, helping Cecil spread those vicious rumors, if you turned me away."

"You are welcome," Gussie said. "Have you had your breakfast? We've got ham and eggs leftover and some nice day old bread."

"I've had breakfast and that buggy out there is filled with food to contribute to the cause. I've brought a bedroll and a change of clothes. I think that's what is needed. I believe we women have got to make a stand or we're going to be downtrodden forever. This is as good a time as any to make it," Myrtle said.

"What about the kids?" Clara asked, thinking of her own three boys.

"I sent them all home. Let their fathers deal with them today. Maybe that will bring them around quicker than anything," Myrtle said with a sly grin on her plain, angular face.

Clara laughed and slapped her thigh. "That's a wonderful idea. Come on over here and let's talk, Myrtle. You know, I'm right glad you stood up to your father and joined us."

"Me too," Myrtle said. "It's not just husbands, you know. It's men in general. Fathers can be testy too when they're wrong and too full of pride to admit it."

In the middle of the morning when the stew pot was bubbling again and the beans were boiling down to make a good thick brown broth, two more women brought their bedrolls and a change of clothing; Cecil's wife, Elisabeth, who declared her husband was the sorriest excuse for a man ever alive and she wouldn't blame Augusta if she shot him between the eyes for his gossiping; and the lumberyard owner's wife, Olene, who was Elisabeth's best friend. Let those two scoundrels who were declaring that all the women in that wagon camp should be beaten, just come down there now with their switches and whips. Olene and Elisabeth brought along a bushel of potatoes and one of carrots, a crate of cabbage and another ten pounds of beans. Elisabeth said if they ran out of one thing, she'd march to the store and take it right from under Cecil's nose.

Clothing flapped on the lines between the wagons, the aroma of fresh food cooking filled the whole area, and the women laughed and visited as they crocheted doilies and collars for dresses they'd make later on. They tatted yards and yards of lovely lace to adorn table clothes or edge out sleeves and embroidered intricate designs on pillow cases.

In town, children demanded services from their fathers that their new mothers had been so adept in giving with loving care. Fathers burned suppers and when they did get something cooked to perfection, the children refused to eat.

Houses began to look like they did before the wives arrived. Flower beds went begging, and husbands slept in cold, lonely beds.

At dusk two little figures came running down the hill toward the circle. Gussie saw them first and was on her feet in an instant. It was her twins and something horrible must be the matter if they were allowed to come to her. Gideon would never allow it, not when he thought she was nothing more than a trollop. Connie stepped in front of her just as she picked up her skirts to run and meet them.

"No," she said. "I'll go. It would be too hard on you and them both to have to separate. I'll take care of it."

"What if Lucy really kicked the window out and jumped?" Gussie whispered breathlessly. "What if she's dying?"

"Then I'll take care of it and come back and tell you," Connie said, leaving Gussie in Berdie's care while she ran out to meet the little girls.

"Hey girls, what are you doing here?" Connie asked sweetly.

"We want to see our momma," Esther said seriously.

"We brung something to her." Ruth held up a roll of wall paper.

"Why did you bring her wall paper?" Connie asked.

"We thought maybe she could draw a picture and write some words to Daddy and then he'd come and take care of his business. Whatever that is. Miss Harris said she wasn't teaching no more school until the men take care of their business. Momma wrote down on the back of the scrap wallpaper about how much to fix the border and some other things, too. We thought she could write on this and then he would come and fix the business," Ruth tried to explain.

"I see," Connie said. "Tell you what, give me that roll and I'll give it to her. We can't let any children come in the camp right now. She says to tell you she loves you very much. Does your Daddy know you are here?" Connie asked, hoping that maybe he'd sent them, that his heart had softened.

"No, he'd skin us. We crawled out the bedroom window and shimmied down the porch post. Abigail is watching for us. When we get back she's going to start screaming. Daddy will run in her room and we'll sneak back up the stairs while he's in there," Esther explained.

Connie bit her lip to keep back the laughter. "Then you run on back home and sneak back inside. Maybe the men will take care of things tomorrow or the next day and by Monday we'll all be back at home."

"I hope so. We miss our momma," Ruth said.

Connie watched them as long as she could. They'd make it back just fine and someday they'd make fine women too. It took a lot of courage and planning for three little girls to conjure up an idea like that, and she admired them for their bravery.

"Is everything all right? What is that?" Gussie met her at the edge of the camp.

"Everything is fine," Connie announced in a loud voice so every one could hear. Then she told the tale of how they'd gotten out of the house and planned to get back inside. "They brought this paper for you to write a message to Gideon on, so that he would come down here and take care of his business. I think I've got a better idea for this paper. Anyone here have a pencil?"

"I do," Myrtle said, pulling one out of her satchel. "I'm a teacher, after all. What are you going to do?"

They stood over Connie who unrolled the wallpaper to find that she had about a four foot section. Mercy, those children must have meant for Gussie to write everything she knew, bringing that much paper. Connie turned it over to the white side and secured all four corners with raw potatoes.

Then she began to write.

Women smiled. Women giggled. Women clapped their hands. Women nodded seriously. It was a work of art.

When she finished, she signed her name to the bottom and handed the pencil to Berdie, who readily added her signature right under Connie's. The pencil was passed back until everyone had a turn. Not one of the ladies turned down the opportunity to add their name to the list.

Later that night, Gussie pulled both blankets up to her chin and watched the stars twinkling out there around the moon. Was it true, like her sister Gypsy had said, that there were secrets in the stars? If there were, could they tell her if her four girls were sad that she was gone. And if they were sad, could God look down and take it away. She'd never want them to be upset.

She missed them so badly, and if she was truly honest, she missed Gideon, too. Sure they fought and had their differences, but he was a good man. A misguided one at times who thought all women should fall out of a submissive mold and walk two steps behind her man with her head down and eyes on the ground, he just needed a little help to understand that there was a new woman on the horizon, one who stayed with her man because of love and respect instead of fear. But deep down inside Gideon was a good man, even if he had jumped to conclusions for which he would never apologize.

It could very easily be a long, long winter before the spring thaw.

Chapter Twelve

On Sunday morning, after another horrible night of soul searching and not liking what he found, Gideon overslept. In all the rushing, he remembered how easy Gussie made everything appear: breakfast on time, girls all looking like dolls from Cecil's store. Gideon missed her. He missed the bantering, the way he felt so alive around her. He wanted her back so bad he could scarcely breathe for the pressure in his chest. He barely had time to get the girls in their Sunday dresses and their hair combed when it was time to go to church. Esther and Ruth complained that they simply couldn't go to church with no curls in their hair, but Gideon assured them that they could and would. Lucy wouldn't eat breakfast, declaring in a voice much too big and clear for a two-year-old, that she wasn't going to eat until her momma came home.

Gideon felt the exact same way. If starvation would bring her home, he'd be more than willing to stop eating. How on earth he'd fallen in love with that saloon girl was a mystery to him, but he had and now he didn't want to live without her and he sure couldn't live with her.

He figured there would be five people in church that morning: he and his four girls. The women wouldn't leave their self-imposed exile and the men wouldn't be speaking to him for causing the problem. But he'd promised that he would show up for church whether the congregation filled half a pew or the church was full with folks standing along the back wall and down the sides.

When he finally had the children in tow and threw open the doors of the church, it was to the sight of one side completely filled with men who looked up at him with eyes as tired as his were. Not one child amongst them looked a whit better than Gideon's girls, who he seated on the front pew where he could watch them, and wondered what on earth he'd preach about this morning. He'd read his Bible until the wee hours of the morning but he had nothing to bring to his congregation.

He waited a couple of minutes before he turned around to face the men. One side of the church was filled to capacity; the other with only four little girls sitting on the front pew. No women and the emptiness was almost as deep as that in his heart. He could well imagine what every man in the whole place was feeling.

"Good morning," he said finally, looking out over them all.

"Good morning, Gideon," Jack said. "We didn't come here for a sermon this morning, and we're going to be right up front and tell you so. We've come to figure out how to end this problem you got us into."

"I see," he said, turning to take his place behind the pulpit, something he came close to taking pride in. The pulpit itself had been constructed of the finest maple wood, sanded and polished until it fairly well shined gloriously. The previous preacher had been quite handy with wood and had fashioned a cross of California redwood which attached to the front of the pulpit. Without a single nail in the construction, the cross was a sign to everyone of the sacrifice Jesus had paid for their sins.

Gideon stopped dead in his tracks. There on his cross was a scroll made from the backside of the wallpaper Augusta had used in his study. Words were written on it, but the fact that it was nailed to the cross with two big nails was what made him see red. How dare any of those women destroy a cross, especially one made expressly for the inside of his church. It was next to blasphemy. His hands shook. If he'd ever been about to try to rectify this error in judgment, the chance was gone now. He wiped away tears as he took two steps nearer and reached out to jerk the nails from the cross.

Something stopped him. Gideon's heart spoke. As surely as if it had a voice of its own it reminded him that the original cross that held his Lord and Savior had two nail holes in it; that the sacrifice Jesus made was for the sins of everyone, and Gideon had sinned when he judged his wife on another man's word. It pricked him soundly when it told him bluntly that he was wrong and everyone in town was suffering for his mistake. And that the cross, albeit a symbol, was just two pieces of wood. The heart he'd broken with his cruelty was a living, beating entity that deserved better.

Gideon read the message written in pencil:

To the men folks of Washington, California. I, Connie Haskell, am writing this with my own hand. Those who are in agreement with it will sign their names at the bottom. We only ask for two things right now. We want Gideon Jefferson to come to the wagon train circle and apologize to Gussie. It has to come from his heart and he has to be earnest in his words. We will expect respect from our men folks from here on out. The other thing is that we refuse to leave our circle until you men folks say that we can sit with you in church. Seems only right and fitting that families are families in church as well as everywhere else. That's all we want.
Connie Haskell

The scroll stopped at the end of the cross and held so many names it made Gideon dizzy to look at them. There at the very bottom was Gussie Jefferson. She'd actually signed her legal name: Jefferson. His wife, and she had to ask for an apology she should have had within an hour of the time when he threw her out of the house.

"Well, gentlemen," he cleared his throat and turned to face the sober-faced men. "I guess this is the ultimatum we've been waiting for. What do you think of it?"

"I think it's time we take care of business," Jack said.

"Hallelujah!" Esther shouted, raising her hand in the air. "Miss Harris said we could have school if you men would take care of business."

"Out of the mouths of babes," Jack said.

"Okay then, after I deliver my apology do we have an agreement over this sitting in church together?" He asked. His heart was lighter than it had been in over a year. "You know the council members discussed this very thing at the conference. They were against it."

"If they don't like it, they can take the church away from you, Gideon. And we'll go down the road and build one that says we can sit with our wives," Sam said. "Seems like a silly rule to me anyway. The women are right. We're families everywhere else we go, so why not in church."

"Okay then, how do we go about this business?" Gideon said.

"I expect you'd better go to the wagons and take care of your part first, and then tell them the other is acceptable," Jack said.

"All right," Gideon said. "You think we ought to make it as formal as they have? I think I do. Anyone got a pencil?"

"Here's one," Ralph said. "Why'd you listen to two old fools like me and Cecil to begin with, I'd like to know. We ought to be the ones down there with our hats in our hands, you know. I'm sorry, Gideon."

"Me too," Cecil said. "Please accept my apologies for spreading such a mean thing. Trust me, it won't never happen again. I think Marlee would skin all the hair off me, roll me in gunpowder, and then giggle while she lit a match to my sorry hide if I ever pulled anything like that again. I was sure wrong."

"The Good Book says for me to turn the other cheek when someone slaps one side. I reckon you slapped me right hard when you told me those lies; then hit me again when you spread it all over town. Now I've turned both cheeks. I can't read anywhere in there where it says for me to let you hit me again. So I reckon if this should happen again that it'll be up to me how I take care of it. I'm going to be up-front and honest. I've not always been a preacher. If anyone slurs my wife or drags her name through mud again I will take my collar off and when I get finished with those folks they won't be able to do such a dirty deed again. So with that in mind, you two, you are forgiven. But your wife and daughter will have to stand behind me next time. If there's anything left of either of you, then they can have it. Understood?"

Both men swallowed a ball of pride no smaller than a good sized cantaloupe as they nodded. Ralph held out the pencil and Gideon took it without smiling. Out to the other side of the long line of signatures he simply wrote: *We the undersigned will meet these requirements. Please come home. We miss you.*

He signed his name and handed the pencil back to Ralph who wasted no time in putting his sloppy name to the list. Jack was next in line and beside Connie's name he wrote "I love you" in addition to his name.

It took thirty minutes for them to sign the paper and then a whole string of wagons and buggies and many men on foot paraded to the edge of the wagon train circle. Gideon carried the wallpaper rolled into a tight little tube and went ahead of the rest of the men. His tongue stuck firmly to the roof of his mouth. The fits Lucy had thrown would be nothing to the tongue lashing Augusta would give him, and he deserved every bit of it. He'd just have to be man enough to stand there and take her wrath, and let his heart break again when she refused to ever come back into his home.

Jack offered Gideon and the girls a ride in his buggy when the crowd dispersed outside. Gideon's hands shook slightly as he held the scroll so tightly his hands cramped.

"So do you really want her back or is this just a temporary thing?" Jack asked bluntly.

"I've done some serious thinking these past days. Even when I was in Sacramento. I've tried denying that I have any feelings for Augusta. Tried my best to think I hated her because of what she was," Gideon said. "It just didn't work though. I'm afraid my heart has better sense than I do, Jack. It's gone and fell for the worst possible choice of a wife that a man could ever have. And now after the way I've treated her and acted, she's probably lost to me forever."

"Try flirting and leaving your shirt off in the evening. Worked for me. Along with a trip to the store for dress goods. I'd sure like to see you two make it work. Connie thinks Gussie hung the moon," Jack said.

"I'm not so sure she didn't," Gideon mumbled.

Viola saw them coming first and knew there was either going to be peace reigning by lunch time or else an all out war was about to be waged. Her own husband stood amongst those on foot who waited at the road's edge. "Well ladies, here comes the general and the troops are ready for action."

Gussie had been washing breakfast dishes. By the time someone poked her in the ribs and pointed, Gideon was only a few feet from her. Lord, he was even more handsome than he'd been before. His hair was combed back but it did need trimming. She'd have to remember to do that before next Sunday. Then she bit her tongue and fought back the tears. She'd be at Connie's even if this was resolved. There was no way he'd ever want her back, not feeling like he did.

"I've brought your scroll back, Connie," Gideon said,

handing the paper to Connie but never taking his eyes from Augusta. That he'd found his voice was nothing short of a miracle. Seeing Augusta in her faded dress shamed him. She was a good woman and just the sight of her rendered him speechless. He should have offered to take her to the store and let her buy whatever she needed to make herself new dresses. The other women in town weren't still wearing faded calico and gingham. He'd failed miserably and he'd go to his grave wondering what life could have been like if he'd been less judgmental.

"And?" Connie didn't smile.

"And you can unroll it and let the other women see it. Augusta would you be so kind as to grant me an audience in private?" he asked.

It was on the tip of her tongue to refuse. To tell him that whatever he had to say could be said in front of her sisters of the heart. But something stopped her. Her heart suddenly had a voice of its own and reminded her that his tone was soft and his eyes were begging as much as his words.

She nodded and followed him to the edge of the river while the women unrolled the wallpaper scroll, held the four corners down with raw potatoes again, and began to read the message, not only from Gideon but their own husbands.

"Augusta, I've come to apologize. What I did and said was unforgivable. I'm not even sure God would forgive such a thing, but I'm asking your forgiveness all the same. That is truly from my heart and I'm sorry," he said, his eyes and the set of his jaw attesting to the fact that he wasn't just spouting off words to get the rest of the women to go home and the men off his back.

She stared mutely at him for several minutes. Was this what her father, Jake, wanted when he sent for his five daughters from the four corners of the world? Was it to ask their forgiveness? How strange that she should think of her father at this time. Even more strange that in that moment, with the sun's warm sun rays dancing around her and Gideon Jefferson that she forgave her father for deserting her. Now could she do the same for her husband?

"Yes, you are forgiven," she said. "I suppose those men are here to take their wives home?"

He nodded.

"Then I'd best get back and help Connie get our things ready."

"Just a minute, please," he said, reaching out and taking her hands in his. "Please come home, Augusta. The girls need you. They're little lost souls without you. Please come home."

"What about you, Gideon? Am I going to go back to the parsonage only to be accused of some other horrible deed in a few days? Are you going to give me a chance?" she asked.

"I'm a hard man to live with," Gideon said. "I know that. I will try to be fair. I need a housekeeper at least until the spring thaw. I'd thought maybe I would write to the girls' great aunt in Arkansas and ask her to come and take care of them for me then. Will you come back now and give me a chance?"

He was asking her to come back as a housekeeper. Never as a wife. He wouldn't go that far, but that would give Gussie four months with the girls; only to have her heart broken at the end of it when the time came to tell them good-bye. She'd have to face that when the time came. If a few months was all she'd ever know of the joys of motherhood, then she'd take it.

His hands grew clammy as he waited for her answer. He couldn't tell her what was really in his heart any more than he could rise up and fly to the moon. The warmth of her hands tingled against his flesh, and he wanted nothing more than to take her in his arms for an affectionate hug.

"All right," she said, looking deep into those big brown eyes of his. "I'll come back to the house. But like before, not as hired help. I'm not a housekeeper, Gideon. I'm Momma to those girls."

"Deal," he smiled.

At the same time a whoop went up from the inside of the camp. Marlee led the shout and the rest of them clapped in unison. The waiting men and children took that as a good sign and swooped down upon the wagon trains like a bunch of bees, hugging and patting their wives, promising to never treat them like Gideon had done Gussie. Happiness filled every corner. When Jack turned the Jefferson children loose they wasted no time in running into Gussie's arms, clinging to her skirt tails and refusing to let go.

"So since you took nothing out of the house, then does that mean you are ready to go home now?" Gideon asked, wishing he still had her hands in his. But that privilege had been taken away the moment she saw Lucy. She'd wrested her hands free and opened them up to the children.

"I need to help clean up," she said, but the men were carting things out of the camp so fast, it didn't look like she was needed at all.

"I think they're happy to have their wives back, and they'll take care of the clean up," Gideon said. "Ready?"

"Let's go home, Momma," Abigail took her by the hand. "I'll lead the way."

"Hey, Gussie," Myrtle called out. "Tell the preacher there will be no charge for the wagons. My father is going to wipe the slate clean on them or I'll come back and camp in this circle by myself."

"Thank you," Gussie called back.

"What was that all about?" Gideon asked.

"I told them this was your fault to begin with so Ralph could put the wagon rental on your bill," Gussie said.

"You did what?" Gideon's eyes, once so repentant, flashed in anger.

Gussie smiled, not knowing which way she liked them best. Repentant was nice, but Lord Almighty that could get old after a short time. Fighting, now that kept her on her toes and alert. If they ever were man and wife in the real sense, she might start a fight a day just so they could go upstairs and make up. She blushed at her own thoughts.

"Seemed fitting to me," she mumbled. "Now girls, did you all have a bath last night?"

"No, we didn't," Esther said. "And our hair has been a mess since you left. Can we take a bath and wash it. We really need it curled for school tomorrow."

"We sure can," Gussie said.

"And can we have pancakes with syrup for dinner?" Abigail asked.

"Yes, we can," Gussie said.

"Anything else you got to say?" She looked at Gideon, walking beside her.

"Not a thing. Right now," he replied.

She fell right back into the role of mother when they entered the house. The kitchen was a complete fright with leftover dishes stacked up from Saturday's supper and breakfast that morning. She put the twins to washing them while she mixed pancakes for dinner; something easy and quick so that she could get them all bathed early and to bed. Then she and the preacher were going to have a set down. She wasn't about to bear her soul and be kicked in the heart again, but she was going to speak her mind without four little girls listening in and worrying about their momma going away again.

"Good pancakes," Gideon said when he finished his dinner. "I don't think anyone is having any at-home socials this afternoon, so I wondered if you girls and Augusta would like a buggy ride in the country. Maybe we'd drive all the way to the mines and let the folks out there meet Augusta?"

Esther and Ruth shrieked with joy. Abigail danced up and down, and Lucy crawled up into Gussie's lap, insisting that she ride in the front with her momma. Augusta didn't think she heard the preacher just right. They'd been living in the same house for more than two months now and he'd never even offered to walk down the sidewalks on Main

Street with her. He didn't even walk across the lawn from the church to the parsonage with her. He'd certainly not offered her a buggy ride. She'd accepted the fact long ago that he didn't want to be seen with her since she wasn't up to his almighty high standards.

"So are you up for a ride in the country?" he asked Gussie.

"I would love it," she said. "Give me time to take off my apron and put on my bonnet. Do I need to get more dressed up than this faded day dress?"

"No, that will do very nicely. Folks out there are a good bit less formal than we are in the city," he said. "I'll go tell Ralph to get our buggy ready and I'll pick all you girls up outside the front porch in fifteen minutes."

The ride was pleasant enough but Augusta kept waiting for the preacher to pull a gun out of his boot and shoot her. Surely he had something in mind other than a nice afternoon buggy ride. If she suddenly dropped dead out there in the wide open country, who'd believe four little highstrung girls when they told everyone their father had killed her? The girls pointed out bunny rabbits and even a family of skunks. Lucy took her afternoon nap curled up in Augusta's lap and using her shawl for a blanket. Everything seemed normal on the surface, but underneath boiled a cauldron of doubts and worries; for both Gussie and for Gideon, who'd realized in the past three days just what his wife meant to him, and how much he'd give to have another chance at making her actually fall in love with him.

Augusta was amazed at the miner's camp. It was little more than a squalor, yet the people there were so respectful and glad for a bit of company. They pumped Gideon for news of the war, asked if he'd brought old newspapers, which he had, and the children ran around free and comfortable with everyone.

"Come on in my shack and let's visit," Clara said after a while. "Gideon, you go on and keep an eye on them babies. Don't be letting them pan today. The water's too cold for them to be playing in. Oh, get that look off your face. I know it's Sunday and you know it's Sunday, but them kids wouldn't know sacred Sunday from washday Monday. I know them oldest girls. They'll be out there in that cold water just seeing what they can see, so you keep an eye on them. Come on in Augusta and let's have a quick cup of tea."

"It's Gussie. Plain old Gussie," Gussie said, stepping into the small one room cabin.

"Honey, there ain't nothing plain about you," Clara replied. "I'm glad to see Gideon has took up with you. He needs a wife and a mother for them children. And he don't need someone who'd let him run over them, neither. Gideon is a bit like that. He likes to have his way, but sometimes it takes a real woman to put him in his place."

Gussie smiled and sipped the tea Clara handed her. So everyone else knew what she'd found out: taming Gideon Jefferson wouldn't be an easy task. Might even take her most of her life to get the job done, but oh, what a good time she'd have doing it. "You must've heard about the trouble we had," she said.

"Lawsy yes, we heard about it. Some of the miners went into the saloons last night and come back telling the tale. What Cecil said and what really happened and all. You girls did the right thing. I was sorely tempted to come into town and join you all myself. Can't imagine how much fun it would be to have a couple of days in a wagon train circle with a bunch of women," Clara said.

"I like your spunk girl. It'll take lots of that spunk to ever change the world, but I think it's a comin'. Thought those men sending for them mail order brides was the oddest thing I ever did hear. Figured they'd be almighty sorry when a bunch of hoity-toity Eastern women arrived wanting servants and maids and real China dishes and all, bringing them out here to this place, but I was wrong. Either you was one tough bunch of women or the trip toughened you up. We're right glad to have your kind in our part of the country."

"Why, thank you Clara. I take that as a compliment," Gussie said. "And anytime you get a hankerin' for female talk and companionship, you come right on into Washington. I'll call some women and we'll take a cup of coffee black as midnight and thick as molasses in my kitchen," Gussie said.

"Momma, Momma, Daddy says we gotta go now or else it'll get dark on us. And I just can't go to school without my hair fixed tomorrow," Esther stuck her head in the door and said excitedly.

"Guess motherhood calls," Gussie set her empty cup aside.

"Never knew it for myself," Clara said. "Maybe I'll just take you up on that offer. I think I'd like comin' around your place."

"I'll look for you. Thanks for the tea and the advice, Clara. I think we're going to be good friends," Gussie said at the door.

"Yep, we are," Clara nodded. And heaven help old Gideon if he didn't watch his manners from now on, Clara grinned. Becky had been a good wife, but Gussie was just what Gideon needed.

All four girls dozed on the way home that afternoon and were more than ready to be bathed in the tub Gussie pulled into the kitchen from the back porch. They didn't even have to be prodded to go to bed, nor did they ask for a story that night. A quick kiss on Gideon's forehead and a big hug for Gussie and they were ready to be tucked in.

"I think we need to visit," Gideon said when Gussie came down from upstairs. "Oh, I emptied the tub for you. I hope you wanted the water poured on that vine growing up the back porch posts."

"Yes, thank you, that is fine," Gussie said. So he had something to say. Well, so did she and she'd gladly go first. "Preacher, I love those girls as if they were my own. I can't bear to see them without a mother and they've adopted me, so what are we going to do about it? There's a war on the wind. You might want to go. You might have to go whether you want to or not. I think I should stay past the spring thaw until we see just what's going to happen. If you go, I'm keeping them right here until it's over. They don't need to be shifted from pillar to lamppost like I was."

Gideon's heart soared. More time to make her love him like he did her. His prayers had been answered.

"I see. I think that is a wonderful idea, Augusta. They do love you and it would be a relief off my mind to know they were with you if I do have to leave to be a chaplain for the fighting men. We voted at the conference that as ministers of God we would not bear arms."

"If that's settled, then I'm going to bed now," she said. "Goodnight, Preacher."

"Goodnight, Augusta. And one more thing: I like the study. It's lighter and brighter and the colors are excellent. You did a fine job. Thank you."

She just nodded, too confused and bewildered to say a word. Had the great preacher just paid her a compliment and thanked her, all in the same breath? There was no way the days of miracles were over. She peeped in on the girls, then shut the door gently to her own room. Her hair pins removed, she washed up in cold water poured from the pitcher into the basin on the wash stand, and then scrambled into the feather bed. She wiggled down into it, pulling the sheets and blankets up to her neck. Gussie Dulan was getting soft, she thought as she shut her eyes. Sleeping under a wagon on the hard ground just couldn't compare to a feather mattress.

Gideon took off his shoes and set them beside his chair. He padded softly upstairs, stopping long enough to peep in on the girls. He wanted oh so badly to do the same to Augusta. Just to look in the door and see if she slept with all that thick hair fanned out on her pillow. To see if she curled up on her side or if she slept on her back. There was a million things he didn't know about his wife. Maybe with patience he would find them all out before he died. It wouldn't be an easy road like he'd had with Becky but it wouldn't be a boring one either. He had a feeling that Augusta would keep him on his toes all the days of his life.

If he could just win back her trust, that was.

Chapter Thirteen

O n Wednesday night Gideon told Gussie that he had a surprise for her planned for the next day. She wasn't to ask questions, but to wear her best Sunday dress the next day and to pack a bag with what she would need to last two days. For the first time since she'd moved into the parsonage she didn't bow right up to him with an attitude, nor did she ask questions. He'd told her to pack a bag for two days for herself. He didn't mention the children so she didn't pack anything for them. Then she went to bed and fantasized about where he might be taking her, until doubts clouded the excitement.

A heavy brick sat on her chest and she could scarcely breathe. They'd had a couple of minor spats since Sunday. On Monday he'd said something snide about her not bringing his coffee to the study and he'd asked her many times to remember it at midmorning. She'd told him that she had just put out a washing, cleaned the whole house which was a mess since she hadn't been there for two days and entertained two little girls while she did it. If he wanted coffee at midmorning, he knew very well where the pot was and the cookie jar was always full. Just help himself and stay out of her way. Good Lord, was he packing her off somewhere on Thursday morning just because she wouldn't serve him coffee? She fretted for more than an hour, then fell into a dream-filled sleep in which Gideon took her to the mines and left her with Clara until the spring thaw. She awoke at dawn, drenched in sweat and shaking all over. Much as she'd enjoyed Clara's forthrightness and company, she didn't want to live like that all winter. It wasn't much, if any, better than living in a covered wagon.

After breakfast, Gideon walked the two older girls to school and came back whistling. Did a good mood mean he was happy because he was finally getting rid of her? Maybe he'd just apologized to give some order and peace back to the town, and was just waiting a few days for the storm clouds to clear before he made his move. That could even be the reason he'd taken her out to the mines on Sunday afternoon; to talk to Clara and make definite plans for Thursday morning.

She had barely cleared the breakfast table and had the dishes done when Connie and Jack knocked on the kitchen door. Gideon jumped up from his chair and greeted them with a big smile and happiness in his voice.

"I didn't tell Abigail and Lucy yet, Connie. Wondered if you could pave the way for me?" He asked so quiet that Gussie had to strain to hear what he was saying from where she stood.

"Have you been nice to Gussie this week? Did you flirt like Jack told you to do?" Connie narrowed her blue eyes and eyed him seriously.

"As nice as a man can be with a wild mountain lion," he whispered.

"Don't try to tame her, Gideon. Just love her like she is," Connie whispered back.

"I'll give it my best shot. Now how about the girls?" he asked.

"I hear you got a trip to go on," Connie said to Gussie. "And I'm going to keep Abigail and Lucy for a couple of days."

"You are?" Gussie asked. "Where am I going?"

"That's a surprise," Connie smiled.

"Connie, Connie," Lucy came down the stairs and threw herself into Connie's arms. "Kittens?"

"Well," Connie hugged the child, "kittens are still there and your Daddy said you could bring one home, and you, too, Abigail. He said two little kittens might be fun to have around since you girls don't get to go to school like Esther and Ruth. But we've got a problem."

"What's the problem?" Abigail asked from the top of the stairs.

"It's a big one," Jack shook his head seriously. "We got five kittens and we don't know which ones you girls might want to bring home. It'll take at least two days for you to look at them and play with them to make up your minds. But I'm afraid you won't want to go home with me and Connie for two whole days. It would mean playing with all of those kittens every day just to see which one loves you the most and would want to come into town and live at the parsonage."

"Lucy can do it," Lucy said seriously.

"Then you think you could kiss your momma good-bye and come home with me for a little while," Jack said.

Lucy nodded her head that she could do that and Abigail agreed from the top of the stairs. Connie asked Gussie if she'd pack them a bag with what they'd need for a couple of days but not to worry if she forgot something because they weren't so far away that they couldn't come right back into town and get it.

Gussie's eyes teared up when the girls kissed her good-bye and rode off with Connie and Jack. It could be the last time she'd ever see them and just the remote possibility terrified her. The preacher had only thought Gussie had fought with him if he had it in mind to get rid of her forever. He'd given his word that she could stay until the war issue was settled and she fully well intended to make him keep it.

"You ready?" Gideon asked.

"No. Who's keeping Esther and Ruth?" she asked. "I didn't pack anything for them."

"They're spending a couple of days with Winnie and Bonnie and Sam is bringing them home this afternoon after school to get what they need. They've whined because they won't have their hair done, but I assured them we would bring them a prize. I told them this morning," he said.

"Then I guess I am ready," Gussie said.

"Then let's be on our way." Gideon picked up their satchels and opened the door for her. Ralph pulled the buggy up to the front porch and Gideon helped her into the front seat like a real husband would do. He drove down Main Street and turned the opposite direction than they'd gone when they went to the mines.

Gussie sighed with relief.

"We're going into Sacramento. It's only a few miles. A nice hour drive and the morning is nice," Gideon said. "A steamship, the *Chrysopolis,* leaves there at ten this morning for San Francisco. I have to do some business with Sutro and Company, which is the investment and banking establishment I use. The boat trip is a little more than five hours so we'll have dinner on it, and dock in the middle of the afternoon. Supper will be in the Rasette House Hotel where we'll stay tonight and tomorrow night. We'll catch the *Chrysopolis* back to Sacramento on Saturday morning and return home to Washington that evening after supper at Ebner's Hotel."

Gussie was speechless.

He waited. And waited. And waited. He'd not known what to expect when he told her his plans. He'd hoped she would squeal with delight and maybe even throw her arms around him in excitement and kiss him again like she'd done that rainy night. Several minutes passed and still she didn't say a word. She was going to insist he turn the buggy around and take her back to Washington, he was sure. She didn't want to spend three days in his presence. Without the children, she wouldn't be there anyway. It was Lucy's cries that brought her back to the platform to marry him, and the girls that brought her back home yesterday.

"Well?" he asked anxiously.

"I'm trying to figure out if I'm awake," Gussie said. "Am I dressed proper for something that big? Why are you taking me with you?"

He smiled. A handsome man already, the smile and the twinkle in his brown eyes made him even more good looking.

"Christmas is two weeks away. I thought maybe you'd like to shop for the girls. And you mentioned a few weeks ago that they needed underthings sewn for them. San Francisco has a much bigger selection of fabrics than either Sacramento or Washington. You can pick out bolts of whatever you think you'll need between now and next summer and we'll have it freighted to Washington. I go into San Francisco twice a year to take care of business matters. So you'll only need to buy what you need for six months at a time. Usually I take the Sacramento Valley Railroad in the morning and come right back in the evening. But this might be a nice trip for both of us."

She couldn't find her voice. The preacher was treating her like a real wife. Going to purchase fabrics and stay in hotels, eat in fancy places. He was going to keep his word after all. She could have hugged him . . . if she'd been brave enough.

"I've never been on a trip like that," she said simply. "Is this already the outskirts of Sacramento?"

"Yes, it is. I was here for the conference," he said.

"You could have come home every night," she said. "There wasn't a bit of need in you staying at a hotel. That had to have cost a dollar a night."

"Three in the place where I like to stay." He grinned. "And I should've come home every night. Then I would've known you were redecorating the study and not entertaining men in the parsonage."

"Amen to that," she muttered, brushing the dust from her

blue traveling suit that was five years old. She would have given most anything to have been dressed in a classy suit with a matching cape and a new hat. The one she wore was as old as her dress and as plain as a mud fence.

They reached the *Chrysopolis,* an impressive side-wheeler, just in time to board. Once underway, Gideon asked Gussie if she'd like to ride on the upper deck so she could see better and enjoy the morning air. The decision wasn't an easy one. She'd enjoyed the cup of tea in the dining room, resplendid with glistening brass lamps and plate glass mirrors reflecting back the images of all the passengers. Watching people all morning while she sipped tea would have been ideal, however sitting on the top deck as they traveled through the water would be an experience too.

"Yes," she finally nodded. "I think I would really like that."

"Then I shall call for some lap robes and we'll go up," he said cordially.

She was still so amazed at the changes in his attitude that she could hardly answer his questions. Perhaps he was truly grateful for her offer to stay and keep the children while he went off to war. It would save him a bundle of his hard-earned gold, after all. He carried the blankets in one arm and guided her through the hallway to the stairs leading to the top of the ship. They were the only ones brave enough to face the chilly air so they had a choice of seats. Gussie chose two where she could see the water flipping over the sidewheels and look at where they were headed instead of where they'd been.

She huddled down under the cozy lap robe and breathed in the nippy winter air, which was nothing compared to what she'd been used to in Tennessee at this time of year. "It's so nice up here," she muttered.

"Yes, it is. What would your weather have been like at this time in the part of the country where you grew up?" Gideon asked.

"Cold. Bitter cold. Most likely with a foot or more of snow on the ground. Wood houses with no plaster or paper inside with the cracks chinked with whatever we could find. I did live with one family for a year though that had the inside all done up fairly nice. Not like the parsonage, but still nice for Tennessee hill folks. What about where you grew up?" she asked.

"Same. The Ozarks can be unforgiving in the winter. Same kind of homes, only more log cabins, chinked with mud. Becky and I had a nice little cabin not far from our church. I farmed some to keep us going," he said.

She nodded. The preacher would never forget his first love. Especially not for a former saloon girl who'd already disgraced him with gossip. Even though it wasn't true, it still lay there like a festering wound between them. She could feel the tension so thick a big old cross-cut timber saw couldn't cut through it.

Sitting, doing nothing but watching the land go by on either side of the water, seemed more like a sin than anything she'd ever done. She thought about her mother and all the relatives she'd known in Tennessee. Jake's people had left that area before she could remember but she did recall her maternal grandmother fussing about the fact that they didn't take any responsibility for Gussie's upbringing. Then her grandparents both died that same year when she was barely in school, and from there she'd been shifted between kinfolks until she was old enough to make her own way. She'd befriended a girl in school who'd gone to Kingsport and danced in saloons. When Ivory came home for a visit, she'd invited Gussie to move to Kingsport with her and she'd get her a job. The rest was history. Her relatives, glad to be rid of her, didn't care what she did as long as she was gone. Then the letter came from Jake, sent to her grandparents and given to an uncle who forwarded it on to Kingsport.

She stole a glance at Gideon whose eyes were shut, but his breathing didn't say he was sleeping. Would she have given him a second glance if he'd come into the Broken Wheel Saloon in Tennessee? He was a very handsome man and carried himself well. His smile, when he bequeathed one of the illusive grins, was absolutely breathtaking. Yes, she would have probably embarrassed herself and missed a few steps in the routine if he'd been sitting next to the stage.

The silence became more and more pronounced between them, then it became comfortable. Gussie remembered something she'd heard about two people finding the right mate when they could sit in comfortable silence for an hour or more. A grin tickled the corners of her mouth at that thought. This morning had been the most comfortable time she'd spent in the preacher's presence. But like all bubbles it would burst at the most inopportune time. They would have an argument because she was oil and he was water. The two did not mix without creating a big mess.

Flirt! Take off your shirt! Jack's voice came to haunt Gideon as he lay there enjoying the morning sun in spite of the nip in the air. He could scarcely throw the lap robe from his body and begin to disrobe right there on the top deck of the *Chysopolis*. However, that might have been easier than flirting. Gideon had no idea how to go about that task. He and Becky were friends before he courted her, then they were married. How did one go about flirting with a former saloon girl anyway? Gideon felt as inept as a thirteen-year-old boy offering to carry home the books of the prettiest girl in the whole school. Augusta would have had so many suitors in her life that anything he could say or do to flirt would most likely just send her into fits of laughter.

"I do believe it's time to be going to the dining room for lunch," he said. "Was that your stomach I heard growling?"

"Do gentlemen ask ladies such things?" Gussie replied.

"I wouldn't know. I guess it's all right for husbands to

ask wives though. I never have researched it in the Good Book," Gideon said.

Gussie threw back her head and laughed. He joined her. For the first time they actually shared and enjoyed a joke, but in his heart Gideon wondered if she was laughing at him or with him. The twinkle in her eye and the way she tossed the lap robe over the back of the chair gave him hope that it was with him.

They had lunch in the dining room. She ordered beef roast with potatoes and carrots, sourdough rolls and a slice of peach pie for dessert. Gideon told the waiter to bring him the same, and added two tall glasses of sweet tea to the order.

"Did you drink when you worked in those saloons?" Gideon asked, unfolding the white linen napkin and placing it on his lap.

"And what would you think if I did?" she asked.

"It's only a question, Augusta," he retorted quickly.

It was him calling her Augusta that fueled the fire of her anger, she decided. She was just plain old Gussie and he refused to use the name even when she'd told him that everyone else called her that.

"Was Becky's name Rebecca or just Becky?" she asked.

"It was Rebecca but I don't see what that has to do with my question," Gideon said, his dark eyes dancing with a touch of anger. So much for a nice pleasant trip. He'd thought they were making progress up there on the deck when they'd passed more than an hour without a spat.

"You used the shortened form of her name but you won't use mine. There was a girl in our chorus line once. Her name was Becky. She had the prettiest blonde hair I'd ever seen. She could have touched her toes to the ceiling if her leg had been long enough. Knew another one in east Tennessee. She was the plainest girl I ever knew, buck teeth, freckles all over her face. Grew into those teeth and a rich man took a liking to the freckles. Married well and settled down to be a banker's wife," she said.

"I still don't understand," he said testily.

"Gussie is my name. Every saloon dancer isn't named Gussie. Nor is every preacher's wife named Rebecca. Why can't you use my name? Why must you call me Augusta?" she asked.

"Gussie was a slave on my uncle's farm. She was a huge woman with big old jowls that hung down and flapped when she laughed. Of all the names in the world, I don't like that one most," Gideon replied. "It sounds cheap and low class."

"I didn't drink," she said. "I never did like the smell of the vile stuff and besides I saw what it could do to families and homes. And Gussie is my name, Preacher. I'm not a slave woman. I don't have big jowls and if you tried, you might be able to overcome that phobia you have about it."

"I could never imagine doing that," he said stiffly.

The waiter brought their food and they ate in silence. This time it wasn't comfortable, though. After a lingering cup of coffee and their pie, he told her that he had ordered a berth for them to take an afternoon rest before docking in San Francisco in the middle of the afternoon. The rest of the day and evening would be busy.

He crawled up into the top berth and she stretched herself out on the bottom one, then he pulled the curtain. It had been months since she'd had time for an afternoon nap. Perhaps she'd spend ten minutes beside Lucy and Abigail humming a lullaby softly until they went to sleep, but to lay down for a whole hour—it was simply luxury deluxe. She wondered briefly what the preacher was thinking about in his berth. Most likely it was that big old slave woman and how much he hated that name.

She shut her eyes, just to rest them for a while. Too much excitement surrounded her to really sleep. The steady rhythm of the ship rocked her gently to sleep as a lullaby played in her mind. The combination of the two didn't keep her from dreaming of the preacher. He kissed her again in the dream, only this time they were in the dining room of the ship. When he opened his eyes, he shuddered all over. The plate glass mirror showed her a reflection of what had caused his revulsion. She was a huge slave woman with big jaws and little beady eyes. She awoke with a jerk to find the preacher touching her shoulder, his face barely a foot from hers.

"We're here, Augusta," he said softly. "You must have been dreaming because you were gasping."

"Guess I was," she said.

She looped her arm through his proffered one as they stepped onto land. A bustling town in the second stages of growth greeted her. He signaled a hackney, gave their bags to the driver, and told him to take them to the Rasette House on the corner of Clay and Grant Avenue.

"So what were you dreaming about?" Gideon finally asked.

Her eyes were everyone at once, drinking in the brick buildings, all the mingling people on the streets. Shops after shops were everywhere. Banks, hotels, merchandisers, even a saloon here and there. But they didn't hold the sway over her that they once had. She'd been a good dancer and trainer of new girls in the business, but she'd gladly never look at another one to be able to keep her new daughters.

"It's so big," she said, ignoring his question.

"Thirty thousand people. Sixty hotels. A public promenade for the social circles. Two artesian wells that discharge seventy thousands gallons of water daily," he said.

"And we can really stay here today and tomorrow?" she asked.

"We sure can. The Rasette House is never full at this time of year. It's my favorite hotel in the city. When we get settled in, we shall go to a couple of shops and then have supper at the hotel restaurant. Then we'll see if there's something in a theater you'd like to see. The Eagle Theater was truly a sight, I've been told. Opened up in '49 but was destroyed by flood three months later. I'd have liked to take you there, Augusta. But there are several others. We could take in a reading or maybe an opera?" Gideon said.

The hotel was even more regal than the ship had been. They were shown to connecting rooms with rose wallpaper, feather beds, mirrors above the vanities, velvet draperies, and brass lamps. Gideon told Gussie that he'd give her half an hour to freshen up and he'd call for her so they could shop for fabrics that afternoon. Tomorrow they'd do the Christmas shopping.

She sat down on the edge of the bed and drew in a deep breath. Her sisters would never believe this. Not even if she wrote them every single detail. She pulled her tapestry bag onto the bed with her and opened it, taking out a comb, brush, and tiny mirror. Her hair was a complete fright, she despaired. She spent most of the half hour refixing it and brushing the dust from the bottom of her skirts.

Gideon knocked on the connecting door one time and then opened it without waiting for an invitation. Gussie was so rattled she forgot to fuss at him for it.

Chapter Fourteen

Gussie brushed her blue traveling suit one more time for supper that night. Gideon knocked on the door at exactly 6:30 and escorted her down to the restaurant where they sat in a candlelit corner table covered with a fine linen cloth. Light gleamed from the prisms on the crystal chandelier lit up from what seemed to be hundreds of candles. Outside, stars twinkled in a velvet midnight sky of pure black, and the moon, a mere sliver of light, glistened.

"So what will you dine on tonight? Seafood, perhaps?" Gideon asked, perusing the menu thoughtfully, all the while wanting to reach across the table and take her hands in his.

"I'm not very familiar with seafood. Maybe you'd order for both of us. I'm not so cowardly I wouldn't try it, I just don't know what's good," she answered honestly.

"We shall have an appetizer of fried clams," he told the waiter. "Then a main course of boiled shrimp and red sauce, steamed rice and perhaps a vegetable medley. Hot rolls with butter and iced sweet tea. Dessert will be ice cream topped with chocolate served with coffee, black as good, thick mud for the lady and very weak for me with two lumps of sugar."

Gussie fell in love with the shrimp and nearly cried when she found out how much it cost. The ice cream was delicious but she felt guilty eating it when the girls didn't have any back home. She was sipping coffee, black as sin and twice as strong, when she heard a familiar voice at her elbow.

"Gussie Dulan, is that you?" a big man with red hair and a drooping mustache asked, his blue eyes twinkling.

"Well hello, Henry. Whatever are you doing in California?" She smiled up at the man. "Join us, won't you? We're just having coffee. Can we order a cup for you?"

"Love to join you, but no coffee. I just ate more than three men should eat. But you'd remember that. You always said feeding me was like feeding a hungry mountain lion after a long winter's sleep," Henry said.

"I'm sorry, let me introduce you. This is Gideon Jefferson. Gideon, Henry Miller," Gussie said. "So tell me, now. What are you doing here?"

"I'm scouting territory for a new saloon," Henry said. "I've got my sights on a piece of property right here in San Francisco and one in Sacramento, too. Want a job?"

"No," Gideon said, shooting the man a look meant to freeze him in his tracks. He reached across the table and covered Augusta's hand with his, the sparks that flew between them startling him. "Augusta was so surprised to see you that she forgot to mention that she's married now. She is my wife."

"Well, slap me on the fanny and call me a newborn." Henry slapped Gideon on the back so hard that Gideon had to swallow quick to keep from spewing coffee all over Gussie.

"Good Lord, Gussie, you said you'd never marry. I woulda stood in the pouring down rain for a chance to propose to you if'n I'd known you was going into the market. So would a lot of the other regulars in Tennessee. You got a good woman, here, Gideon. I sure hope you appreciate her. She can train up a floor show out of nothing but green rookies in a week. Give her two weeks and she'll have them doing a show that'll pack the house fuller than church on the last night of revival."

"Thank you," Gideon said. "I'm quite sure I did get a good woman."

Well, slap me on the fanny and call me a newborn, Gussie thought.

"So where do you two live?" Henry asked.

"A little community called Washington a few miles from Sacramento," Gussie replied. "Gideon has four lovely little daughters, so I stay too busy to think about saloons any more."

"Well, you ever change your mind and want a job, honey, you just put out the word in any saloon that you're lookin' for Henry and I'll come runnin'," he said, pushing back his chair. "I'll leave you two with your coffee, now. It sure was good seeing you again, Gussie. Never did catch that last name. Was it Johnson?"

"No, Jefferson," Gussie said. "Gideon and Gussie Jefferson."

"Good night to you both. Like I said, Gideon, you got the best Tennessee has to offer. Treat her good."

"Do my best," Gideon waved.

When Henry was out of hearing distance, Gussie let out a long gasp. "Thank you so much for not telling him you were a preacher."

"So, you ashamed of me being a preacher?" Gideon's hackles raised up, jealousy and anger mixing to unsettle the pleasant evening.

"No, I am not, but Henry wouldn't have believed it. Then he would have stayed forever. He was the owner of the saloon down the street in Tennessee where I lived. Always trying to hustle me to come to work for him. It would have just been awkward, that's all," she said.

"Well, far be it from me to make an awkward situation for the almighty, wonderful saloon dancer who can train a string of girls in just a week," he said coldly.

"You didn't miss a word, did you?" she asked, her tone as frigid as the ice cream she'd just eaten.

"No, I did not," he said. "Are you ready to go up to bed?"

"Is that a polite question or an invitation? Polite question, yes I am, alone. Invitation, don't even think about it," she said, rising from her chair and starting off ahead of him without even looking back.

He followed her out of the dining room, across the lobby, up the stairs, and down the hall to the suite he'd rented. She was a mixture of honey and vinegar. Sweet and lovely one second, sour and aggravating enough to provoke a saint to sin the next. Why, oh why had he ever let his heart fall in love with the woman? *Love!* The word terrified him so bad he stopped breathing for a minute, then he gasped. How could he love Augusta? He did care deeply for her; want to keep her as a wife since she kept the house running smoothly and the children happy. But love her? Want to snuggle down in the bed with her at night?

"What brought on that sigh of disgust?" She turned on him so quickly that he'd already taken two steps forward and they literally collided right in front of her door.

"Nothing. Just a fast trek up the stairs. Did anyone ever tell you that you sure walk fast when you are mad?" Mercy, she smelled like roses and her chest planted against his felt so good he didn't want to ever step back. His arms went out instinctively around her waist and then up to her neck.

The kiss was sweet at first, then deepened into a lingering one that Gussie never wanted to stop. When he drew back, she slipped her arms around his neck and brought his mouth down to hers one more time. Yes, it happened again. That itchy feeling down deep in her soul, too deep to scratch, too deep to understand. That mushy, warm sensation down in the pits of her stomach. It must be what had drawn Willow to Rafe and Gypsy to Tavish when they were so mismatched.

"Ahem." Gideon stepped back until they weren't physically touching, yet their emotions were still weaving binding cords from one to the other. "Good night, Augusta." He pulled the key to her door from his pocket and carefully unlocked the door.

"Good night, Preacher," she said.

He threw himself across the bed when his shaking hands had opened his own door, and stared at the connecting door between the two rooms. There was no lock on it. He could open it up right now and stroll across the room, take Gussie in his arms and make her a real wife. From that second kiss, he didn't think she'd stop him. But he couldn't. Not until he examined those crazy feelings she'd evoked in him.

The door flew open and she stood there in her nightrail with a shawl wrapped around her shoulders. Her golden brown hair hung down her back, and those strange blue eyes flashed.

"Thank you for a wonderful afternoon and supper. I can't begin to tell you how I've had such a good time. I still can't believe all the money I spent today. The fabrics we picked out are lovely and I can hardly wait to get home and start sewing for the girls as well as for myself. And I do not walk fast when I'm mad," she said bluntly.

"Yes, you do." Gideon raised up from the bed and held his hands behind him to keep from reaching out to touch the soft skin on her neck.

"No, I do not." Gussie took two steps closer and wrapped her arms around his neck. She only had to raise up slightly on her toes to bring her lips up to meet his. The third time was supposed to be the charm. If the world didn't stop moving, it would do it on the third try.

It wasn't the charm. Everything sped up, rather than stopped, when they kissed. The whole world swirled into a vacuum that held only the hearts and souls of Gideon and Gussie Jefferson.

"Now goodnight, Preacher. Breakfast at seven?" she asked, leaving him standing there in awe.

"Breakfast at seven, and you're welcome," he said.

She shut the door softly and stumbled across the room to the bed. Not able to talk her jelly-filled knees into another step she fell across the bed and shut her eyes. She was in love with the preacher. Not just in like with him. Truly in love with the man. She didn't want the kisses to end. She wanted to curl up in that big bed with him and become his wife.

When had it happened anyway?

She went back to the first day when she married him and replayed as much of every day as she could. She never could put her finger on an exact time. It had just happened and there it was in bright colors right before her face. She loved the preacher and he was still in love with his wife. She could fight a flesh and blood woman who had faults and failures, but she could never fight a perfect angel. Even if she did have her own faults when she was living, they'd been buried with her and all the preacher remembered was the wonderful things about her.

Gideon pulled the sheets and quilts up to his chin in a physical attempt to cover up the emotions raging in his body and heart. He couldn't actually, really, love Augusta because it would disgrace the memory of his first love, Becky.

"Becky is gone. Go home and put those pictures in the girls' bedrooms. They need to remember their mother and Augusta won't begrudge them a bit of that. Matter of fact, she's the one who takes them to the cemetery to visit Becky's grave anytime they want to go. She encourages them to remember little things about her and savor them for their own. No, Augusta won't resent the fact that I loved Becky first. She's not that kind of woman. Like Henry said, she's the best Tennessee has to offer," he whispered to himself.

Not able to sleep, he paced the floor. Finally, he'd had all he could endure. He'd tell Augusta right now and they'd talk about the fact that he'd fallen in love with her. He eased the door open and was in her room, ready for her to jump out of bed any moment and whip him with that caustic tongue of hers. But she was fast asleep, curled up on her side with one hand under her cheek.

Gideon sat down in the rocking chair and simply watched her sleep for the better part of two hours. He couldn't wake her, yet he couldn't leave. He needed to tell her how he felt and ease the heaviness from his heart; yet he couldn't have done it even if he could awaken her.

Beautiful, was all he could think. Augusta was beautiful, lying there with the pale light of the night dancing through the lace curtains on the window. She was passionate, head strong and opinionated, and would probably change the world before she left it. But she wouldn't depart without making sure her mark had been made.

He could either accept that and love her like she was, as Connie had whispered, or he could forget Augusta. Invisible soft hands reached inside him and loosened the cords around his heart. While he sat in the darkness with his shirt off, all the scars from the past fell from his heart as if they were chains and had been unlocked.

Gideon wasn't ready just to love again, he was ready to love Augusta. Tomorrow he would tell her so. He went back to his room to pray earnestly that he hadn't read too much into those three kisses that wasn't there.

Chapter Fifteen

Gussie felt out of place at the investment company while she listened to figures beyond her comprehension, but when Gideon asked for papers to change the beneficiary to all his wealth from his sister in Arkansas to his wife, Augusta Jefferson, she suffered the first case of vapors she'd ever known. It took all the willpower she could drag up to keep from falling right out of her chair into the middle of the finely polished wood floor.

"Why did you do that?" she asked when they were back in the carriage and Gideon gave the driver and address on Washington Street.

"Because if you are to raise my daughters should something happen to me in the war, then I want to know you have complete access to my money, Augusta. Besides, I want you to know how much money there is so when you go to Cecil's, you won't worry about what you are spending," he said.

"Thank you."

"You are very welcome. My sister in Arkansas is a practical woman but if you have the responsibility then you shouldn't have to have her assent before you spend a dime. Besides I trust you with the money. You wouldn't build a saloon and teach them to dance, would you?" he asked, a glitter in his eyes.

"No, I would not!" she exclaimed. "Why would you ask a question like that? My girls aren't ever going to have to resort to such things. They'll be loved and taken care of proper and they'll be wanted."

Gideon threw back his head and laughed harder than Gussie had ever seen. A soft giggle began in her, but soon she was laughing right along with him. He threw his arm around her shoulders and drew her close to his side, wrapping the lap rug around them both. "I know you wouldn't do that, Augusta. If I didn't trust you I wouldn't have signed those papers."

"Thank you, again," she said. She didn't inch away from him when the laughter died down, but enjoyed sitting in the closeness of a public embrace. Was this what marriage was really like? Was it more than arguing and going to bed alone for sleepless nights? Maybe it was sharing jokes, talking about the future, sitting close in a hired hackney and being kissed passionately several times throughout the day.

"Now why are we going to Washington Street?" she asked.

"W. H. McNalley's place. He sells plows, seed harrows, churns, cheese presses, and that kind of thing. Jack asked me to purchase alfalfa and chili clover seed for him. He's going to plant it in the spring. It's supposed to stay green and grow from six to eight weeks longer than any other grass and it reseeds itself so Jack will only have to plant it once every six years or so. He wants to run a few more head of cattle next year. There's a market for beef all up and down the coast. Not that he'll have to go far. Restaurants in Sacramento, San Francisco, Folsom, and all of Yolo County will buy anything he can produce," Gideon said. "And Cecil gave me an order for McNalley to fill. They'll ship it all to Washington and it'll be there the first of next week."

"I'd like to look at the churns. I didn't find one in the parsonage and I really like to make my own butter. I could also use a cheese press," Gussie said.

"Then we shall have them both. You just pick out what you want," Gideon replied, enjoying the feel of her body so close to his.

By lunch time they'd visited the McNalley store and two dry goods establishments where Gussie took her time choosing fabrics for little girls' dresses, underthings, and even two bolts of pure soft cotton for Gideon's shirts. She ordered two dozen new preacher's collars and several spools of thread, yards and yards of commercial lace, and buttons by the dozens.

"And what for you?" Gideon asked when they were back in the hackney where he'd given the driver instructions to take them to a restaurant on some street Gussie had never heard of.

"I'll pick up something at Cecil's," she said.

"I don't think so."

They dined on chicken salad sandwiches, hot homemade noodle soup, and crusty bread slathered with butter in a small corner restaurant that wasn't nearly as fancy as the one in the hotel, but the food was so good and Gussie was so tired and hungry that she didn't even look at the surroundings. After she satisfied her raging appetite, she planned a long afternoon nap curled up in that soft bed in her hotel room.

When they'd flagged down another hackney, Gideon gave the man an address which certainly was not on the corner of Grant Avenue and Clay. Gussie almost sighed with disappointment, but he'd been so nice all morning, she couldn't utter a word of protest. The driver took them into an area of town that looked richer than where they'd just come from. The people on the streets were dressed fashionably. Ladies strolled in gorgeous hats and dresses of every color, adorned with bustles and bows in the back. Gussie noticed matching capes trimmed in fur or velvet with hoods hanging down their backs, and fine lace trims on everything, instead of homemade crocheted edgings. Her eyes, suddenly wide awake, took in everything as fast and furious as she could. She wished for a sketch book so she wouldn't forget anything. Miniature capes like that would be so cute on the girls for Sunday morning. Bustles were out of the question for her, though. She couldn't imagine sitting on a pillow. Why, sure as shootin', she'd fall off the thing right in the middle of church services and there she'd be sitting sideways, looking for all the world like a drunk trying to make it home, with one leg on the sidewalk and the other on the ground.

The driver stopped in front of a store with dresses displayed in the windows. The windows were so clean and polished that it looked like a woman could reach out and touch the rich-looking clothing. Thinking that Gideon had read her mind about trying to memorize details, she scarcely blinked as she stored away every detail of a dress in a pale aqua blue that came close to matching the Dulan girls' eyes.

"Shall we?" Gideon hopped out of the buggy when the driver opened the side door and held his hand up to Gussie.

"Oh, Gideon, thank you. I've been trying and trying to capture all the little things about the dresses I've seen, but they were going by so fast," she said.

"Fast? Augusta, did you know that right here in San Francisco a man has built a flying machine. A Mr. Richardson who says his machine will travel at least eighteen miles an hour and he's planning on giving a demonstration in a few months." Gideon took her arm, looped it through his own and escorted her to the windows.

"Are you teasing me about a flying machine?" she asked.

"No, I am not. Someday I fear that man will fly through the skies like birds in some kind of flying machines. It's a scary idea, isn't it? Already we're building railroads that will take people from one side of this continent to the other in less than a month's time. That's mind-boggling, isn't it?"

"Yes it is. But not as mind-boggling as that dress right there. It's lovely," Gussie muttered, giving all her attention to the dress in the window. "If only I could find lace like that, I think I could reproduce it."

"I don't think so," he said.

"Preacher, there is nothing wrong with that dress," she flared up. "It's decent. The color might be light for this time of year, but it's not flashy."

Gideon just smiled and opened the door to the store, standing back to let her enter first. "Let's go inside and really take a look."

"But—" she started to protest so he took her hand and pulled her inside the store.

"I am Gideon Jefferson," he said to the proprietor. "This is my wife, Augusta. She would like to try on that dress in the window if you have it in her size. And do you have a cape to match it. Maybe one with some fur around the edges and on the hood? Then we'd like to see a few more things in her size so we could choose two or three new dresses. Maybe a discrete dark blue and a burgundy. I think she'd look lovely in a deep maroon."

Gussie's heart stopped beating. It literally quit right there in the middle of the fancy California dress shop.

"That's too much," she whispered to Gideon. "Did you see the price tag on that dress? I could make the girls a wardrobe for what that costs."

"And you shall make them a wardrobe, I'm sure. Many, many times before they are grown women, Augusta. You can make your own day dresses and work clothing, but from now on you shall have three new dresses twice a year for church and for your Ladies' Auxiliary meetings," Gideon whispered back.

"Yes, we do have it in her size," the lady returned with the dress from a back room. "And I found three in dark blue and two in maroon, the lady might want to try on also."

Gussie tried on and modeled the dresses for Gideon, who nodded his agreement on two of the blue ensembles, the aqua from the window and a deep maroon that gave a permanent flush to Augusta's cheeks. She'd never had more than three store bought dresses in her whole life combined, much less in one day. Now she had to decide between the two dark blue outfits. She repaired her hair in the floor length mirror in the dressing room and carried the maroon dress out to the sales lady. She'd give Gideon the job of choosing which blue one his money was about to purchase.

"The dresses will be delivered to our hotel this afternoon," Gideon said. "I've taken the liberty while you were in the dressing room of ordering hats to match them. I hope that's not overstepping the boundaries of a husband. Time is slipping away and we should eat an early supper if we are to catch that piano performance I promised you tonight. It starts fairly early for an evening show."

"That's fine," Gussie said, her head still reeling from the shock of spending so much money in just one day.

A waiter escorted them into the dining room as soon as they arrived back at the hotel. Gussie's stomach was in such turmoil she didn't figure she could eat a single bite of food, but when they brought a platter of fresh steamed shrimp, her appetite returned with gusto.

After supper, Gideon escorted her to her room, told her to choose whichever new outfit she liked best and be ready to go to the opera in an hour. "Personally, I like that maroon one for this event," he offered stiffly. "It brings out the color in your cheeks and makes your hair look absolutely lovely."

"Well, thank you, Preacher." She blushed. It seemed that all day she'd been thanking him. When she looked back over the day, it amazed her that they hadn't fought more. Maybe when married people had short little trips and spent lots of money, they didn't fight.

She laid her worn traveling suit on the rocker beside the window and dressed carefully in the maroon dress she found hanging in the wardrobe with the other things they'd bought that day. She'd had a hard time deciding on which blue traveling suit to purchase so Gideon had simply waved his hand at the sales lady and told her to wrap up them both.

Gussie dressed in record time and then opened the wardrobe doors so she could sit in the rocker and stare at the new dresses and hats. When she heard Gideon close the hall door to his bedroom, she carefully shut the wardrobe and pulled on a pair of black leather gloves that matched the black fur trim on the cape and the hem of the maroon dress. She could never wear something this fancy to church or to the Auxiliary meetings. It would have to be saved to wear when they came to town during the winter months for Gideon to do his business with the investment company.

She opened her door before Gideon had time to knock. He was glad he'd seen her in the outfit before that moment because if he hadn't, it would have taken his breath away and he would have behaved like a teenage boy with his first crush on a pretty girl.

"You are looking lovely, Augusta," he said formally, reaching to help her with the cape and then tucking her arm into his. "The recital tonight should be delightful."

Mercy, he had just paid her a compliment and had something positive to say at the same time. A sheer miracle had just happened in the halls of the Rasette House Hotel and yet most people didn't even know a thing about it. She wondered if that wasn't the way of all miracles. Only the people involved were touched by them.

"It seems, Preacher, that I've been saying thank you all day long. But I'll add one more to it, and say thank you for such a gracious compliment. I'm excited about the recital. Did I tell you that my sisters Velvet and Garnet both were piano players? Garnet even more than Velvet. Velvet played in church while Garnet played a wild saloon piano," she said.

"And did you dance to that music?" Gideon asked.

"Oh, no," Gussie exclaimed. "I didn't even know Garnet in those days. She grew up in northern Arkansas. I grew up in Tennessee."

"I forgot that your sisters weren't acquainted until Jake died," he said, leading the way down the hall and staircase. Once in the hackney, he pulled the lap robe over their legs and gave the driver directions to the theater.

He couldn't remember a time he'd enjoyed as much as today. Every nerve in his body was alive and the mere touch of Augusta's gloved hand on his arm sent his senses reeling. Remembering the kisses the night before put a silly grin on his face that made him very glad it was dark and she couldn't see it. Nothing could possibly go wrong from here on out. Oh, they'd fight and fuss; that was their nature. But soon, very soon, they'd be man and wife in every sense of the word. And Gideon was looking forward to it with passion.

They were inside the foyer of the theater fifteen minutes early. Gideon led Gussie up an enclosed staircase to a box that he'd requested. High up, with only four other people, she should be able to enjoy the recital even more than if she'd been sitting on the ground floor amongst so many people. Gideon sat Gussie in a padded chair of light blue velvet in a balcony box with deep blue velvet curtains tied back with gold tassels. The stage was right below them and she could see the shiny black piano waiting for the lady's hands to bring it to life. Everything was perfect. Gussie was a queen sitting high on a throne and not one thing could go wrong.

"Well, hello again," Henry said, taking a seat in the box with them. Six seats in one box and of all the people in the world, two of them were to be occupied by Henry and his lady friend. "Please let me introduce you to Amanda Nelson. Amanda, this is an old acquaintance from Tennessee, Gussie Dulan. I'm so sorry I've forgotten your married name."

"Jefferson. Gussie Jefferson, and this is my husband, Gideon Jefferson," Gussie said.

"I forgot to ask," Henry said, properly seating Amanda,

"do you have a saloon in the town where you live beside Sacramento?"

"No, I do not," Gideon said, glad he'd decided against wearing his minister's collar that night.

"Oh, hello!" The curtains parted behind them and a third couple bustled in. "Well, imagine this. Gideon I didn't know you were in town. Suppose it is that time of year when you come to San Francisco. But imagine meeting you here?" Floyd said.

"Hello, Floyd," Gideon said through clenched teeth. "Let me introduce you to my wife, Augusta. And this is an acquaintance of hers from Tennessee and his companion for the evening, Amanda Nelson. This is Floyd Adams and his wife, Clair. They are from Sacramento."

"And he's a preacher," Henry said, a wicked grin on his face.

"Yes, of course," Clair said. "Are you also a preacher?"

"Oh, no, lady," Henry chuckled.

"And you are from Tennessee, Augusta? What a surprise? We weren't even aware that Gideon was courting anyone much less already married. This comes as a great surprise to us all," Clair said.

"Yes, I'm from Tennessee," Gussie said. "Gideon waited until after the wedding, I'm sure, to make announcements."

"But I just saw you last week and you didn't mention it," Floyd said, seating Clair next to Gussie.

"I guess I didn't," Gideon sighed.

"You never did tell me what it is you do if you don't own a saloon?" Henry asked.

"A saloon!" Floyd's eyes came nigh onto popping right out of his head.

"Why not?" Henry asked. "It's an honest living."

"Oh, my." Clair began to fan so fast the little feathers on the edges of her fan looked as if they were going to fly away. "Did you know Gideon through his station while he was in Arkansas?" She asked, hoping to change the subject.

From now on she'd have Floyd make sure just who they would be sharing a box with.

"No, I didn't know Augusta until the wagon train of brides came from St. Joseph, Missouri. I was the first one to choose a name from the hat and I chose Augusta," Gideon said.

"Well, I'll be hanged from the nearest oak tree," Henry said. "So that's the way you got out here?"

"That's the way," Gussie said, pride filling her chest because Gideon hadn't hidden behind a subterfuge of lies.

"Then you never knew him before that moment?" Clair asked, suddenly more intrigued than was really right in the sight of the Almighty.

"No, I did not. As a matter of fact I almost didn't marry him because he was a preacher," Gussie said.

Gideon jerked his head around to fall into the depths of her blue eyes which were twinkling with mischief. She'd just admitted to Henry that she married a preacher and actually seemed proud of the fact.

"And I sure came close to calling off the marriage because she was a former saloon dancer. There she stood in that red shiny dress with all this black lace and I was so full of pride and judgment that I was sure enough judging the book by the cover," Gideon said, never blinking. The preacher who was the backbone of the conference in California and the saloon owner didn't exist anymore. He and Augusta were the only people in the box.

"Well, she thought it was beautiful," Gussie said.

"And it was," Henry boomed. "You should have seen her kick up her heels in that dress in Tennessee. I offered to double her salary just to steal her away from the place she worked. But she's a loyal woman and wouldn't quit the man who'd given her a job when she needed it."

"I'm aghast," Floyd stammered. "You should have discussed this with the conference, Gideon, before you made a decision like this."

"Did you discuss it with the conference when you married Clair, Floyd? Did you drag out every little thing about her past and put it up for review? I don't think you did," Gideon responded.

"Well, it sounds like to me that we're all in business to help each other," Henry patted them both on the back. "I'll provide a place for the men to sow their wild oats on Saturday nights. And you can provide a place for them to come and pray for a crop failure on Sunday morning. Now let's watch this performance."

"Let's do," Amanda said. "I do love the piano. Play it myself. Henry and I are discussing a job in that line."

Gussie choked back a very unladylike chuckle and sat through the whole performance even though she wanted to plead a fake headache and go back to the hotel. Talk about a crazy situation. Henry and Amanda sitting in the same box with two preachers and their wives. Floyd and Clair were bound to be on their knees praying for redemption until the wee hours after sharing a concert box with a saloon owner. Gideon reached across the arm of the chair and took Gussie's hand in his sometime during the performance and she didn't yank it free.

Floyd didn't listen to a single note in the recital. He didn't like these kind of things anyway and he'd only come to appease Clair. But he'd thought through the whole situation. Next week he'd call a special meeting of the conference. All but Gideon would be invited, and they would give his church to a new man, one worthy of the station. They'd give him thirty days to clear out of the parsonage. If he wanted to order a mail order saloon dancer and marry her then that was his business. Remaining a preacher at the Washington church was Floyd's. Clair, who'd been about to faint, stole looks at Augusta who was still a blushing, beautiful bride, and was already devising an excuse to drive over to Washington in the next few days so she could get to know this woman better. Henry couldn't wait to get back to Tennessee and tell all the people there that Gussie Dulan married a preacher man, while Amanda was hoping that the relationship with Henry developed into more than just a business agreement.

And two hearts that couldn't say a word on their own spoke to each other and said all the things that lay between a man and his wife. Gideon determined in his heart that he would speak his mind when they got back to the hotel. He wasn't waiting another moment. As soon as he and Augusta had a private moment he was going to tell her that he'd fallen desperately in love with her. Gussie, her hand held firmly in the preacher's, could hardly wait until they were back in their rooms. She was going to burst through that door again and have another kiss or two. She became light-headed and ignored the music just thinking about it.

Finally, the last applause died down. Each couple said their good-byes and Gussie and Gideon were back in the hackney for what seemed like the thousandth time that day. At the hotel, he ushered her up the stairs, his hand on the small of her back and coming nigh onto setting her skin on fire even under all the layers of fancy clothing.

"Good night, Augusta," he said at the door, a bit stiffly, but refusing to lay his heart open out there in the hallway.

"And to you, Preacher," she said, just as formally.

He threw his coat on the bed and untied his tie. If he'd been a drinking man, he would have thrown back a couple of shots to bolster his courage. But he was a preacher, so he bowed his head and asked God to give him the strength to say the right words.

She threw her cape on the rocking chair and removed the fancy hat with black lace around the crown. If she'd been a drinking woman, she would have tossed back half a bottle of cheap whiskey to prop up her courage. But she was a preacher's wife, a former saloon dancer, who never liked the smell of any kind of liquor. So she searched deep inside her heart and asked God to give her the strength to open that door and walk into what she hoped would be the preacher's open arms.

She had the door knob in her hand when it turned from

the other side, flew open and there stood Gideon in all his handsome glory. "I was coming into your room to tell you that I love you," she said bluntly and simply.

"And I was coming into your room to tell you the same thing." Gideon said as he grinned.

"What are we going to do about it?" she asked.

"We got one more night in this hotel. I guess we could call it a honeymoon," he suggested, wanting to reach out and take her in his arms.

"But you aren't going to sleep with a saloon dancer," Gussie reminded him.

"And you aren't going to sleep with a preacher. I think the words were that you'd kill me if . . ." he said, the last words ending when she wrapped her arms around his neck and kissed him.

"I'm not a saloon dancer anymore. I'm your wife," she said breathlessly when the kiss ended.

"I'm not wearing my collar tonight. Tonight I'm simply your husband," he said, enveloping her into a hug so close he could hear her heart doing double time.

"I love you Gideon," she said, pulling his face down for another kiss.

"I love you, Gussie," he said, hugging her tightly before he tipped her chin back to taste her lips again.

"I think I just found the promised land," she muttered, resting her head on his chest, listening to his heart beat entirely too fast.

"I know I did," he agreed in a soft whisper.

Epilogue

The photographer set up his equipment in the middle of a riding arena. His subjects sat on stair-step seating that still smelled like brand new lumber. The owner of the horse operation, Tavish O'Leary, had told him earlier that he and his brothers-in-law had built that seating arrangement especially for this picture. However, it would be a wonderful addition to his arena. Now visitors would be able to sit and watch the training sessions. They might stay longer and buy more horses that way.

Gussie and Gideon climbed to the top of the four rows of seats with their brood of children. The oldest should grace the top of the mountain, Gypsy had said. To which Gussie shook her finger at her younger sister. Gussie arranged her billowing skirts after she'd sat down just off center stage, and patted the seat next to her. Her husband, Gideon, sat down close to her and threw his arm around her shoulders. He informed the four young women who were their daughters that they would sit beside their mother; the husbands of the three older ones would sit beside their wives; and Lucy next to her mother. The four boys would sit beside him.

179

California was well-represented on the top row of the seats. Gideon had a church in Broderick, which had changed its name from Washington. Not the original church where he preached when he first married Gussie, but a community church with no denominational name attached to it out at the edge of Broderick. They didn't have Sunday school, but the women and men sat together, and Gussie taught a youth group on Thursday nights. Esther and Ruth both brought husbands and two children each. Lucy was going to the University of California studying to be a lawyer. Heaven help those opposed to the women's rights movement when she passed the bar. Willam and Duncan, twins, sat beside their father. Eighteen-years-old and already in their second year at the university. Grant and Jacob sat beside them. They were sixteen and fourteen with eyes the light aqua color of their mothers.

On the next row, Gypsy organized Velvet's family on half the row and Garnet's on the other half. Velvet had come from Laramie, Wyoming where her husband, Hoyt still had a thriving medical practice and an even more thriving ranch. They brought three sons with them: Jake with clear blue eyes like his grandfather had had and who was already his father's right arm in the ranching business; John, eighteen, and leaving from Coalville, Utah to go to Louisiana next week to study to be a doctor like his father; and little Andy, four years old, the tag-along his mother said, and the son who'd stolen her heart almost as much as Hoyt had twenty years ago.

Garnet's family took up the other side. From Winnemucca, Nevada, which had started out as Frenchman's Ford, she'd brought her husband, Gabe and their children: two daughters with red hair and light eyes. Grace, who'd be married to her sweetheart when they got back home to Nevada, and Jane, who was the school teacher in Winnemucca, at least until the end of next school year when she planned to marry the banker's son. One son, Gabriel, was fifteen and declared he was going to grow up and be a lawman like his father had been at one time before he gave up his star for his many varied businesses.

On the bottom step, Gypsy instructed Willow and Rafe, with their brood of children, to have a seat. Six boys and one girl who kept them all in line. Rafael, Jack, Cyrus, Henry, Harry and Beau, ranging in age from nineteen to twelve, and Emily, the daughter with dark hair and eyes the exact color of her mother's. She was sixteen and one look from her was all it took to quiet that six-pack of ornery brothers. They lived on a farm in Nebraska and in a few years she had full intentions of going to college to study art. The boys would all most likely be farmers and ranchers just like they'd been trained to be.

On the second step, Gypsy sat down and Tavish joined her. Two girls took their place beside their mother; two beside their father. They all had hair as black as a raven's feather. Two of them had Dulan blue eyes, two had Tavish's clear blue eyes. They lived and breathed horses and Tavish was proud of his family of girls.

In a row of chairs below the bottom step, Gypsy had told Annie and Hank, and their children to be seated for the picture also. Merry had come along with her husband and four children. She'd married Rafe's nephew when she was eighteen and they ranched right next door to Rafe and Willow. Annie and Hank's sons, Jake and Mark, sat on the other side of Hank.

Silver sprinkled the Dulan girls' hair those days but the picture didn't show it. It just portrayed a whole family of happiness that day during the first family reunion they'd had. It was held at the O'Leary horse ranch in Coalville, Utah which had started out as Chalk Creek. After the whole family photograph had been taken, Gypsy arranged each family on the green grass for a picture of them individually. The last picture was one of her and her four sisters, sitting on the grass in a circle.

"Just like the circle of wagons where we really got to know each other," she said.

"Here we are, Jake Dulan. Just look what a family you produced!" Gussie exclaimed.

"Smile and hold it for a minute. Don't blink," the photographer said. Five lovely women with the most gorgeous eyes he'd ever seen, sitting with their skirts billowed around them on the prettiest green grass in all of America and a blue sky behind them. He hoped he lived to see the day he could make a picture that would show all the colors.

They smiled and didn't blink.

"Well, did you find the promised land?" Gussie asked the other four.

"Yes, it's in the middle of Nebraska and that stagecoach driver was dead wrong about there not being a promised land." Willow grinned, a few wrinkles showing around her eyes these days.

"No, ma'am, it's right here in Coalville, Utah," Gypsy said. "You should all four move here so we could be closer."

"Gotta disagree," Velvet said. "The promised land is in Laramie, Wyoming. That's where you've got to go to find it."

"No, it's in Winnemucca, Nevada and I'm already homesick to see it again," Garnet said in a low whisper, the result of nearly dying at the end of a hangman's rope.

"I think the promised land is anywhere the heart is happy. My paradise is in Broderick, California," Gussie said. "I hope our father has found an eternal promised land. I hope he's happy wherever he is and that he knows we are friends as well as sisters."

"Thank you Daddy Jake for bringing us together and setting us on the path that brought us to our own promised land," Gypsy said.

"Amen," the other sisters said in unison.

A soft wind blew across their faces that afternoon and somewhere down deep in their hearts they each knew without a doubt that Jake Dulan was at last truly resting in peace.